I0721492

BURN THE NIGHT

THE ENFORCERS

JANE HINCHEY

BAYWOLF PRESS
BP
BAYWOLF PRESS

Burn the Night
The Enforcers #1
Copyright © 2020 Jane Hinchey

Cover Art Design by Jacqueline Sweet

All rights reserved. No part of this book may be reproduced or used in any way without written permission from the publisher except as permitted under the Copyright Act 1968.

This is a work of fiction. Any likeness to actual people or events is purely coincidental. Unauthorized use could spark the wrath of supernatural forces—or worse, land you in a steamy romance you never saw coming!

Burn the Night/Jane Hinchey - 2nd ed.

AUTHOR'S NOTE

Welcome to "The Enforcers" series—a collection that has truly been on a remarkable journey. When I first embarked on this adventure, I could hardly have imagined the twists and turns it would take. Initially self-published under my own name, these stories found a new identity with the pen name Zahra Stone, and even underwent a title transformation along the way. Now, they've come full circle, returning to their original author.

While I'm predominantly known for my cozy mysteries, "The Enforcers" holds a special place in my heart. It's a series that has evolved with me and witnessed the various stages of my writing career. I'm thrilled to present these stories to you once more, enriched by their journey and under my own name again.

To stay updated with all my literary escapades, including the latest on "The Enforcers" and my cozy mysteries, I warmly invite you to sign up for my newsletter. It's the best way to keep in the loop about new releases and exclusive content.

You can sign up for my newsletter here:

Janehinchey.com/subscribe

Thank you for joining me on this incredible journey. I hope you enjoy the world of "The Enforcers" as much as I have enjoyed bringing it to you.

xoxo

Jane

ABOUT THIS BOOK

I'm Raven Black, an SIA paranormal investigator, and my latest case is a dive into uncharted waters. Mutated humans are just the tip of the iceberg. Alongside my partner Carter, I'm tracking a shadowy scheme to engineer a new breed of supernatural beings. In a world where the uncanny is commonplace, this feels darker, more dangerous. And as we dig deeper, the heat between Carter and me is hard to ignore.

As we chase leads, confront formidable foes, and unravel a web of dark secrets, our lives and future teeter on a knife's edge. Along the way, I discover startling new powers and truths about my origin that turn my world upside down.

Balancing my emerging abilities with my growing feelings for Carter is a tightrope walk. As the stakes skyrocket, I'm thrust into a role I never imagined, standing at the forefront of a battle against a sinister plan.

With every moment fraught with peril and passion, I must harness my full potential and trust in the bond Carter and I share. Will we extinguish the looming threat before it engulfs everything? Can our love endure the trials we face?

'Burn the Night' is a high-octane blend of supernatural thrills and sizzling romance, where every choice could be the difference between triumph and disaster.

Author's Note: Embark on a revamped voyage with 'Burn the Night,' the tale you may have once known as 'Born in Fire,' penned by me, Jane Hinchey. For a time, it walked the world disguised as Zahra Stone's creation, but now it's returned home—newly polished, substantially edited, sharpened, reforged, and ready to bewitch once again under my true name. It's been quite the journey, but the best journeys often are.

The city was a wash of neon and rain, the latter coming down in relentless sheets, turning my bones to ice as I pounded the pavement. Not far ahead, the perp zigzagged through the streets, but he wasn't shaking me—not tonight. My breath puffed out in steely clouds as I matched his every turn, my determination as unyielding as the downpour. I was gaining ground, legs pumping, lungs heaving. Ahead of me, he turned another corner. Stupid mistake. I knew this city like the back of my hand, and my friend ahead had just turned into a dead-end alley. Seconds later, I swung into the alley behind him, skidding to a halt when greeted by his growl.

He was trapped, his back to the wall, and the

displeasure was evident in the snarl that twisted his features. His lips pulled back, revealing teeth too sharp to be human. A werewolf, without a doubt. He gestured with a jerk of his head, a silent dare.

"Ready to go a few rounds, loser?" he challenged.

I couldn't help but roll my eyes. "That's your line?"

"That's the line."

I stood relaxed but alert, one hand nonchalantly resting on the grip of my pyre gun. With a flick of my wrist, my trench coat billowed slightly, intentionally showcasing the SIA badge clipped to my belt. His sneer deepened—he clearly wasn't intimidated.

"You? With the SIA?" He practically snorted the words. "You're no more paranormal than the man on the moon." His nose twitched as he sniffed, his senses searching for something in my scent that might betray fear or falsehood. He wouldn't find either.

I shrugged, unfazed. "Look, I'm not here for small talk. It's raining cats and dogs, I'm drenched, and I've got a warm shower and a hot coffee with my name on it. So, let's wrap this up, shall we?" I didn't wait for his reply; his next move spoke volumes.

He lunged in a blur of fury and fangs. But I was quicker—my reflexes honed by more than just training. "Stop right there!" The words were a mere formality. My power surged forth, slamming into him with the force of an unseen wall. He was frozen, quite literally, caught between forms. His leap had begun with a transformation—man to beast—but my intervention had him hanging in limbo, part human, part wolf, utterly immobile.

Fingers dancing along my belt, I found my cuffs, swinging them with a flourish that matched the smirk on my lips. "Tough luck, buddy," I quipped, snapping the metal around his half-transformed wrists with a satisfying click. Reciting his rights in a matter-of-fact tone, I was smugly triumphant we had another rogue off the streets. A slight press against my wrist and the comms unit buzzed to life. "Package wrapped. Alley off Main and Magnolia."

"Copy that, en route," Carter's voice, ever calm, crackled back.

Another stray raindrop dared to slip down my neck, an unwelcome shiver against my skin. With a grunt, I yanked up my collar, a futile barrier against the night's damp assault.

Headlights sliced through the drizzle as our SUV rolled up, the rhythmic thump of wipers keeping time with my pounding heart. Carter hopped out, his stride purposeful as he approached us. He secured the collar around the werewolf's neck with practiced ease and retreated. Withdrawing my power, I watched as our perp collapsed to the ground, the groan he emitted mingling with the hum of the idling engine.

"See, sugar, all that could have been avoided if you'd just stopped when I asked you to," I told him sweetly, patting him on the head. With the silver cuffs and collar, his transformation had receded, and he was back to his human form. Changing from man to wolf was painful: bones broke, organs rearranged themselves. To be frozen mid-change just prolonged the agony because when you were on the receiving end of my "gift," you could feel and hear everything. You could still breathe and sometimes speak; you simply couldn't move. "Not supernatural?" I quirked a brow. "Guess again."

Carter hauled the wolf-man toward the SUV, his arm a vise around the perp's shoulders. As he wrestled him into the back, the reinforced silver bars of the custom cage gleamed a warning in the dim light—no ordinary slammer, this one. My gaze flicked over the setup, a silent salute to the SIA's ingenuity. Funny how it took the top brass twelve years and a parade of red tape to realize their handcuffs were paper thin against the supernaturals. Humans had been playing catch-up ever since we blew our cover, a quarter-century revelation that had them reeling. Now, as the door clanged shut, sealing him away, there was a grim satisfaction in knowing we were the ones keeping the balance—not them.

Water from my coat pooled on the passenger seat as I settled in, the storm outside punctuating the moment with a clap of thunder. The heater's hum was a welcome sound, and I stretched my fingers toward its promise of warmth.

"Nice work back there," Carter remarked, a lopsided grin on his face as he navigated us out of the alley.

"Thanks. You weren't too bad yourself," I replied, acknowledging his earlier success with a nod.

He had been busy, too, rounding up the rest of the wolf pack while I was engaged in my own dance. Back-up had already carted them off to HQ.

Carter's features tightened as he spoke. "It's a sick game they play, a human hunt."

"The humans don't stand a chance," I agreed.

The voice from the back cut through our

exchange, jarring and unrepentant. "We buy them fair and square!" our captive insisted.

I whipped around, fixing him with a glare. "Buy humans? You're not seriously suggesting—"

He smirked back, all bravado and misplaced pride. "I'm not suggesting anything. I'm stating a fact."

His silence after that was as thick as the tension in the SUV. Carter and I exchanged a look that didn't need words. There was a market for humans, and we had just scratched the surface.

THE DAMP COAT clung to my frame like a second skin as I collapsed into my chair in an unceremonious flop. My hair, drenched from the night's downpour, hung limply around my face. With the perp securely locked up, the night's adrenaline ebbed away, leaving me with nothing but the chill that seemed to seep into my bones.

Carter peeled off his jacket with a methodical ease and took up residence at his desk. Four stories below the bustling streets, the SIA facility was a symphony of modernity, where every surface gleamed with purpose, and every device hummed with quiet efficiency.

The air, filtered and circulated with silent sophistication, carried a faint, engineered freshness devoid of the city's cacophony of scents. It was a bubble of technological purity, an oasis of calm insulated from the chaos above.

"You look like you've been dragged through hell and back," Carter remarked, his eyes taking in the smudges of fatigue that were the only color on my otherwise pale face.

"It's been one of those nights, you know?" I gestured aimlessly, my exhaustion manifesting in my half-hearted attempt at humor. "I can manage without the coddling, Carter."

"Someone's gotta do it," he shot back. "You're not exactly a poster child for self-care."

I scoffed, leaning back in my chair. "Hey, I've been on my own since I was practically in diapers. I can handle a little rain and a late night."

But Carter knew the score. I had no family, no maternal figure to cluck over me. I was a product of the state—Raven Black, a name as on the nose as it was a constant reminder of my beginnings, an orphaned babe left in the care of nuns. My life had been a series of temporary homes and even more temporary attachments until the streets became my home.

Carter, with his infuriatingly charming penchant for meddling, had slipped into the role of my protector, the knight I never summoned yet found myself begrudgingly reliant upon. It was that look in his eyes, a blend of concern and something else, something that sent an unexpected shiver down my spine—a shiver that had nothing to do with the cold.

His gaze lingered a little too long; the corners of his mouth twitched with a restrained smile, speaking a language our banter never touched. Sure, he worried, but beneath that, there was a pull, a silent acknowledgment of the electric current that thrummed between us, as palpable as the storm outside.

I wasn't just any lone agent—I was Raven Black, self-reliant, self-assured, and more than capable. I'd built walls as high as the ones that housed the rogue supernaturals we hunted. Yet, here was Carter, finding cracks I hadn't patched, glimpses of vulnerability I didn't voice.

He'd taken it upon himself to become my watchdog, but the truth was, Carter wasn't just watching out for me. He was watching me, always one step too close, his presence a constant warmth at my back. And as much as I'd never admit it out loud, his nearness sparked a dangerous dance in my chest, tempting me to lean into the heat, if only to stave off the chill.

"Raven," he sighed, scrubbing a hand over his face.

I rolled my eyes at his concern and cut him off before he could wrap me in cotton wool. "So, selling humans, eh?"

He let his hand fall, and his fingers found the keyboard instead. I sprawled in my seat, watching him take the bait, the workhorse to my slacker.

"Coming up empty," he grumbled. "We're gonna need to cozy up to Redmeadows PD for their missing persons list."

I righted myself, a cascade of water from my hair pooling on the floor. Logging in, I began searching our recent cases that involved humans turning up dead. If humans were being shopped around, there was a system, a sick cycle of capture and sale. Did the hunters mark the prey first or just snag whoever was convenient? I wagered the former—it had the stink of 'organized' all over it.

Those reported missing within a day of turning up dead, I tossed aside. In our twisted world, a missing person was a dead person—supernaturals didn't kidnap, they hunted. And in their twisted game, humans were nothing but pawns, morsels. It always led back to the bloodsuckers, with their thirst and their cloaks and their drama. But a gnawing suspicion crept in—what if the wolves were playing a game of their own, a shadowy hunt no one saw coming?

TWO

The sun was peeking over the horizon, painting the dawn with streaks of yellow, orange, and pink as I pulled into the underground garage of my apartment building. The twelve-hour shifts at SIA were killers, but rogues didn't work the same hours as humans. Most activity was between seven in the evening and seven in the morning, necessitating two twelve-hour shifts a day. We rotated on a two-week basis: two weeks of nights, two weeks of days, and four days off between shift changes.

Slinging my bag over my shoulder, I crossed the parking garage to the side door that led directly into the foyer, stopping to check my mailbox before taking the elevator to the third floor. The building was an old hotel originally built in 1912 that had been renovated into boutique apartments. I'd bought my two-story, two-bedroom place three years ago, and I loved it. Twelve-foot ceilings, hardwood floors, exposed brick, granite and stainless-steel kitchen, luxury spa bath, and a skyline view blocks from the river. My apartment was my refuge from the world, and I guarded my privacy with great zeal and a state-of-the-art alarm system.

Disarming said alarm, I dropped my bag on the coffee table by the door and leaned down to unzip my boots. Breathing a sigh of relief, I kicked them off, leaving them where they fell by the front door. Padding to the kitchen, I grabbed a popsicle from the freezer and headed upstairs, unzipping my jacket as I went. A narrow walkway ran the length of my apartment's upstairs area, consisting of two bedrooms with a gorgeous-sized bathroom sandwiched between them. Besides my bed, my bath was my favorite place to hang out. Placing the popsicle on the wooden stool next to the tub, I flipped on the faucet, leaving it to fill as I stripped off my clothes on the way to my bedroom.

There she was, my goddess of a bed, a magnificent creation of wrought iron with a white tufted headboard. The covers were a mess, a tumble of white comforter, silver sheets, and bronze pillows. I rarely bothered making my bed, a small rebellion against the years at the orphanage and the rigorous rule we were under. I tossed my clothes on the old armchair in the corner, where they hung precariously on top of the bundle of clothes already there. Stepping out of my underwear and unsnapping my bra, I tossed them in the laundry hamper. Okay, I admit it, I treat my underwear with more respect than the rest of my clothes. I'm hooked on matching sets, any color, lace, push-up, bandeau, you name it, I have it in my collection. It's my secret little pleasure the rest of the world doesn't need to know about.

Hitting the remote for the stereo, an electro-pop beat holding a hint of darkness filled the room. I pinned my hair into a messy knot on top of my head and cranked the music up louder, dancing around the room, losing myself in the music, gyrating down the hallway to the bathroom. My reflection in the bathroom mirror caught my eye, and I stopped for a minute, examining myself critically. At five foot eight, I was leaning toward the tall side of average. Thanks to years of training with the SIA, my body was fit and lean, my skin was paler than I'd like, but then I was either working nights or inside a lot of the time, so I didn't get to spend much time basking in the sun's glow. I could see why the nuns had called me Raven. My hair was jet black, so dark that in places where the light hit it, you would swear it had indigo highlights. My brows were equally dark, as were the thick, long lashes I'd been blessed with. Everyone got distracted by my hair, but I thought my eyes were my best feature. Not just green, but an emerald green, and with how thick my lashes were, it looked like I permanently wore eyeliner.

I'd copped a lot of shit from the other kids when growing up. I was pretty, and I attracted a lot of attention because of it. Then they discovered I was different, and the attention changed into something darker, uglier.

Filling the bath with hot, scented water, I eased myself in, flexing a foot to flick the taps off. Neck resting on the rim, I leaned back, staring at the ceiling as the steam wafted around me. As the steam rose, I sank deeper into the bath, the heat coaxing the tension from my muscles—a luxury I never took for granted. It was a memory seared into my senses, the first time I had ever bathed in a tub. I was twelve, a temporary fixture in yet another transient home. I remember slipping into the water; the sensation was transformative, starkly contrasting to the biting sprays back at the orphanage. That first touch of warmth was a revelation, a balm for more than just the flesh.

But that sanctuary was short-lived. The daughter of the house, a girl with eyes like storm clouds, resented my mere existence, my intrusion into her family. One night, her envy, silent and sharp, manifested in scissors glinting in the moonlight. I woke to locks of my hair, as dark as raven's wings, scattered across my pillow—a crude shearing driven by fear and jealousy.

Her fear became tangible when, in my half-asleep haze, my fury took hold, an untamed force that I barely understood myself. She floated, suspended, a rag doll in the grip of my rage. The house erupted into chaos, her screams a siren calling the parents. Their faces, pale and wide-eyed, spelled the end of that chapter.

I never saw that bathtub again.

Shaking the memory, I realized the bath had cooled, and the memory clung to me with a shiver. With a flick of my toe, the plug popped free, and the water began to gurgle down the drain. I wrapped myself in the towel, drying off; I finished my popsicle and slipped into bed, naked. I couldn't be bothered wearing nightclothes; I tossed and turned so much I always ended up so tangled they cut into me painfully, pulling me awake. I closed my eyes to the sound of the city around me—traffic starting to hum outside, voices, the noises of a world waking up. I was used to sleeping during the day. The day-to-day of everyone else's life had become my white noise. With a sigh, I let slumber take me.

THREE

"C'mon, Black." Carter handed me a coffee. "We don't wanna be late."

I followed him into the briefing room. Most of our colleagues were already there, chatting amongst themselves while they waited for the briefing to start. I slid into a seat, sipping on my coffee.

"Mmmm, this is good." I heard Carter chuckle and looked at him from the corner of my eye. Such a handsome guy with a heart of gold to boot. Plus, he bought me coffee. I'd offer to marry the sexy bastard, but I wasn't a wolf, and he was. Not to mention, I had plans for my future, and marriage wasn't one of them.

Silence fell as the director stepped into the room

and took her place behind the podium. She was a stunning woman, tall, slim with hair a gorgeous shade of red. She wore black slacks, stilettos, and a sheer white button-down blouse with a matching camisole beneath. She oozed elegance and sophistication, but I also knew she had ovaries of steel. You didn't want to mess with Keri Ridgeway, Director of the SIA, not if you knew what was good for you.

"Agents." Her voice rang out, clear and strong. "We have another body matching that of the three we have found over the last month." She raised her hand to shush us as groans rang out. "I know. This is not a good situation. In fact, it's very, very bad. The fourth body has the same characteristics as the first three, and that is, it is deformed or mutilated from the inside out. The victim is Allena Niles, nineteen, a student studying medicine at Redmeadows University. She worked part-time at the Witches Brew Restaurant as a waitress. At first glance, we can't find any connection between her and our other three victims."

With a click on the podium, the screen behind the director lit up, revealing a virtual case board.

"Victim one, Tara Dewitt, twenty-two, a grade school teacher. Her car was still at the school, indicating she'd been abducted from there and her body dumped in an alley. Not hidden, so the perp wasn't too bothered with her being found. Victim two, Brad Headley, twenty-five, an accountant. His car was found in the parking lot of a supermarket. Video surveillance shows him paying for his groceries and leaving the building, carrying two bags. His body was found in a dumpster, no sign of the groceries. Victim three, Kimberley Shay, seventeen, unemployed. She'd just finished school and was taking a gap year. Her last movements have been difficult to track. We're still trying to nail down who saw her last and where. And again, she was found in an alley next to a dumpster."

I leaned forward, focusing on the photo of the last victim, Allena Niles.

"Niles's body was found in a disused warehouse at the old end of the docks. Her injuries are the same, but the dumping of her body has gone against the pattern."

The director was silent for a moment, letting us take in and ponder this latest piece of information. Why the different location for the body dump? I raised my hand.

"Black?" The director indicated I could speak.

"Who found the body?"

"Couple of kids playing at the docks. Found an unlocked side door and decided to explore. Scared themselves shitless at what they found. The Guardians were first responders and secured the scene. Their report is available with the rest of the case file." She indicated the electronic data displayed on the wall behind her. "This case is a priority, people. We're going to have the Redmeadows PD, and God knows who else breathing down our necks on this one." She looked out over the group of SIA Agents in front of her, considering.

"Carter and Black, I want you two to focus on our latest victim. Trace her movements and get down to the morgue. We need autopsy results ASAP. McConnell and Richards, to the warehouse, see if the Guardians have missed anything. Augustine and Darabi, find the connection between the victims. We must stop whatever 'this' is before humans swarm the place, holding us up. Get to it."

Back at my desk, I swiped my hand across my screen, enlarging the image of the dead woman Allena Niles. Her body was twisted and contorted in a non-human way; her face screwed up in a picture of agony. I hurt just looking at her. It was as if she was partway through a change, and it all went horribly wrong. I wasn't a werewolf, so I'd never experienced the change, but Carter was, and he told me it was excruciating to begin with. All the bones in your body broke and re-set as your body transformed into your wolf. The whole process took around five minutes for newer wolves, and the older you got, the faster the change. You also couldn't control when you changed. Unless you were Alpha. Alphas could change at will, the rest of the pack only at a full moon. And the full moon wasn't for another couple of days.

I leaned to the right, peering around my screen to catch Carter's eye opposite me.

"Coming?"

"Definitely." He wrinkled his nose as he rose. I knew he didn't like visiting the morgue and that the scents were overwhelming for his sensitive nose. He wasn't the only one.

Pulling on my Kevlar jacket, I zipped it to my chin. Kevlar suits were standard issue in the SIA, and I was grateful for the added protection. Dealing with vampires and werewolves could turn into a bloody business, and I didn't favor having my skin ripped open. Kevlar prevented that. It was also an extra incentive to keep in shape. The pants were much like yoga pants, skin-tight and molding every curve. The jacket hugged my body, allowing freedom of movement without restriction, the zip running from my waist right up to my chin to protect my neck, the sleeves long enough to loop over my thumbs and protect my wrists. A utility belt slung around my hips, an extra band around my thigh to hold my gun holster. Steel-capped knee-high boots and a comms unit around my wrist completed the uniform.

I looked across at Carter, who'd just finished strapping his gun in place. The male uniform consisted of Kevlar combat pants, boots, and a jacket similar to mine. I pulled on my cap, pulling my ponytail through the loop at the back to swing down my back. I couldn't help but grin. Together we looked pretty badass, all in black, with a red SIA badge clipped to our belts and printed on our hats.

The morgue was housed in the SIA Science and Medical Facility across town. Supernaturals rarely needed medical assistance, but now and then, they did, and laws that prohibited humans from treating us had been passed. I fell into the supernatural category even though no one knew what I was— including me. I had to submit to medical testing when I applied to join SIA. According to blood test results, I had one hundred percent human DNA. Yet, I could freeze everyone around me within a twenty-foot radius with a flick of my hand. It was a nifty trick, holding someone in place, unable to move. I didn't know how I did it. I just did. And I didn't understand why, even though paralyzed, they still breathed, but they did. Sometimes, I froze them up so hard they couldn't speak, but I mainly hampered movement. And because of that particular talent, I'd been classified as supernatural, species undetermined.

Initially, they thought I was a witch, but even witches couldn't do what I could, and I didn't need to cast a circle or spell, so I was pretty sure I was not a witch. I could feel their magic, though, and I liked it, so I lived on the edge of Witches Quarter, where their magic wrapped around me, comforting, warm. Some speculated that I was a cross between breeds. Yet, I exhibited no werewolf or vampire traits, let alone shifter or ghoul. I'm an anomaly.

Snagging a set of car keys from the board and clocking us out, I stepped into the elevator behind Carter. Rather than going down, we went up. SIA offices were six stories below ground, and each floor housed different ranks of the SIA. Level six, the furthermost down, was our holding cells. Level five was the Guardians—think corporals in human terms, officers who'd completed their training and were fresh into the agency. Level four was the Enforcers—think detective in human terms. Carter and I were Enforcers. Level three is the executive floor where the SIA Director had offices, plus IT, payroll, and finance staff. Level two is the Protectors —think sergeant. How good you were determined how quickly you got promoted up the ranks. Then on level one were the Cadets and training facility. The lift opened into the basement of a high-rise car park. Twelve stories of car parking above us, six stories of Supernatural Investigation Agency below.

I climbed into the driver's seat and turned the key in the ignition. The engine roared to life with a throaty growl, and I had to admit, I liked driving the beast. It was big and heavy and drove like an angel. I flipped on the lights and eased us out of the parking lot. Early hours of the morning meant little traffic in downtown Redmeadows. We'd make it to the Science and Medical Facility in ten minutes with no traffic snarls to slow us down.

Redmeadows was dissected by the Amuletic River, a massive river running nearly two thousand miles that passed through Redmeadows on its way to the ocean some hundred and twenty-five miles further north. Along one side of the river were mountain ranges, and Redmeadows had been settled at the foot of the mountains in the eighteen hundreds. The SIA Science and Medical Facility was squeezed between the docks and Wolf Hill. The SIA didn't require much land as most of their buildings expanded underground, and the Science and Medical Facility was no different. A one-story building, with the ground floor housing a reception and waiting area and half a dozen private meeting rooms. The facility's science lab, medical wing, and morgue were below ground.

Pulling up in the open parking lot, I killed the engine and stepped out. Carter was talking on his comms unit to his mom, who was doing the "mom" thing and trying to set him up with a nice wolf girl. He was deflecting. I watched as he scrubbed at his face in annoyance. One thing I'd learned about wolves: they seemed obsessed with reproduction. A lot of pressure came from their pack to settle down and start producing pups as quickly as possible. I didn't understand it; their species was not in danger of becoming extinct. Carter had tried to explain to me that pregnancies were difficult and dangerous. Often the mother or baby, sometimes both, didn't survive. I still didn't get it. If it was so dangerous, why were they so keen to pursue having kids? I shrugged, some species I'd never understand.

"Look, Mom, I gotta go. I'm on a case." He disconnected the call and looked over at me with a sheepish shrug. I wished I could sympathize, but having no parents meant I had no one trying to set me up. Or look out for me. Or love me.

"Let's go."

I'd never liked the morgue; it was a library of the silent, where the stories had unwelcome endings. The cold was a tangible presence, an uninvited companion that clung to my skin and seeped through my clothes. The overhead lights hummed a monotonous lullaby, unnaturally loud in the silence.

Carter stood beside me, his warmth a stark contrast to the chill of the room. I could feel his eyes on me, heavy with concern. He knew something was off, could probably sense the way my powers bristled at the proximity of death.

A geeky-looking lab tech, all gangly limbs, and shy nods, logged us in. "Shifter," Carter's murmur brushed my ear. I shot him a look. His uncanny ability to read my mind could be extremely annoying at times, but on this occasion, I was grateful. Unlike Carter, I couldn't just sniff the air and determine what type of supernatural a subject fell under. Turns out our tech was a shifter. Not that it mattered.

The tech slid out the metal tray with its shrouded burden. "Allena Niles, nineteen, Redmeadows University med student," he recited, clinical and detached.

Snapping on a pair of latex gloves, the sheet fell away at my touch, revealing Allena's tragic transformation halted mid-shift. Her face was a grotesque tableau of the wolf she never became. Bones jutted where they shouldn't, skin translucent and fragile as a moth's wings. I carefully lifted one arm and examined it. It looked pretty normal, except for her fingers, which were broken, and her nails looked like they could have been transforming into claws. I examined her other arm, pausing when I got to her hand.

"Look at this." I motioned to Carter, who stepped forward.

There was a faint mark on the back of the girl's hand.

"Is that a—?" Carter frowned.

"I think it might be." I nodded, looking at the lab tech who'd also moved forward. He handed me an ultraviolet flashlight and killed the main lights. As soon as the ultraviolet light hit the girl's skin, the marking became crystal clear.

"Crimson Mist?"

"That vamp nightclub in Mistlyn, on the other side of the river," Carter explained.

"Did the other victims have this stamp?" I asked the lab tech.

"Couldn't say. The skin on their hands was too degenerated. I can run some tests, see if I can find any ink trace."

"Do that. Let us know immediately if you find anything."

FOUR

We had a lead. That was more than what we had with our other victims. The first three were found dumped in various locations around town. Nothing tied them together except for the horrific way they had died.

"So, our victim number three, Kimberley Shay, was last seen leaving her waitressing job at The Witches Brew, that restaurant in the Bell District."

I nodded. "I know it. I've been there often." The Witches Brew was within walking distance of my apartment. The Bell District was one of Redmeadows' tourist haunts, full of art galleries, restaurants, and bars. A colorful district that attracted locals and visitors alike.

"What time did she leave work?"

"Ten p.m. Plenty of time to hit a nightclub after work."

"Next?" I prompted.

Carter checked the screen he'd activated from the dash, linking us to the central database, "Tara Dewitt. Twenty-two. Last seen at the school where she teaches eight-year-olds. Her car was still in the parking lot. Either she was snatched there, or someone picked her up, and she left her car at work. Doesn't make sense, though. If you're going out and don't want to drive, you'd take your car home first."

"Agreed. Next?"

"Brad Headley. Twenty-five-year-old accountant. He was last seen leaving the office, but his car was found in the supermarket car park."

"Video surveillance from the supermarket shows him shopping, paying for his purchases, and walking out the door. Cameras don't extend to the car park." Carter continued.

"And his groceries weren't found?"

"Nope. Footage shows him walking out with two bags. Neither he nor the bags were seen again."

"Back to Allena, our latest vic. So she was what...nineteen? Twenty? Uni student?" I tried to recall what I'd already been told.

"Nineteen. Studying medicine at Redmeadows Uni. Once we get back to the office, I'll start tracking her last known movements. That stamp could be a couple of days old."

The ride back to HQ was silent, a backdrop to the whirring of my thoughts. The change in the body's locale was a nagging puzzle. Sure, our perp was a fan of the ol' dump and dash, but a forsaken warehouse? It was a new move. Before, hiding wasn't part of the game—bodies were left in plain sight, a brazen challenge. But this? This was a shadowed corner, a place where secrets could slumber undisturbed. It begged the question: Why the shift to the shadows? Why now? And more importantly, how? That was the million-dollar question.

How was the perp morphing full-blood humans into... what? Monsters? The autopsy reports were a jigsaw puzzle with pieces that didn't fit—human blood tainted with a cocktail of DNA. Cross-contamination? Unlikely. These changes were a bizarre fusion of vampire and werewolf—fangs meant for the night paired with the snout of the wild, skin as pale as moonlight with patches of unusual hair growth. A supernatural chimera that defied any logic. It was a puzzle that didn't just bend the rules—it broke them.

Back at my desk, I shrugged off my Kevlar jacket, hanging it on the back of my chair. Removing my pyre gun, I dropped it into the top drawer of my desk, followed by my hat. Stripped down to my Kevlar pants and black tank, I looked more like I was about to go jogging rather than an SIA agent. With a flick of my wrist, my black hair cascaded down, sending a waft of my scent towards Carter. His reaction was instant, a sharp breath that cut through the silence.

"Raven," he growled, his voice a mix of warning and desire, eyes locked on me with an intensity that bordered on the primal. I ignored the flutter in my stomach, sliding into my chair with an air of nonchalance.

"You know," I said in a conversational tone, activating my screen rather than looking at him, "my last name is a bit on the nose. Raven Black. It's like they ran out of ideas after looking at me."

He managed a terse chuckle, even as he stripped off his gear. "It suits you."

I didn't dare look at him; those chocolate eyes were a temptation all their own. His scars, his rugged features—they added to his allure, made him more than just a pretty face. And with the full moon on the horizon, every line of his body seemed to thrum with a wild energy.

"Stop it," he snapped suddenly, breaking the spell. "Your thoughts are loud."

I shrugged, feigning innocence. "Sorry. Can't help it if you're broadcasting in HD."

A taut smile played on his lips. "Just... be careful."

Careful. The word echoed in my head, a reminder of the line we hadn't crossed. But oh, how we danced on it.

Turning my attention back to my screen, I typed in Crimson Mist Nightclub and clicked the link to the club's official website. Owned by Nate Wilder, managed by Xavier Elizondo. The website didn't reveal much. A listing of guest DJs and events they had coming up. Humans and supernaturals welcome. Beverage listings, including synthetic blood. Crimson Mist was located in Mistlyn, on the south side of town and east of the Amuletic River. Mistlyn's old loading docks and cobblestone streets hinted at the former warehouse district's past, while stylish bars and gleaming lofts pointed to its modernization. Crimson Mist was on the waterfront, one of the converted docks. Prime location. It must have cost a pretty penny.

A report notification appeared in the top right-hand corner of my screen. I bookmarked the Crimson Mist web page and closed the browser, enlarging the incoming report with a swipe of a finger.

"Yep. Just like we thought, Carter. Body dump. Allena Niles was not killed at the warehouse where she was found. Looks like the kids who found her got in the same way as our killer, the broken door on the west side of the warehouse. Tire marks right outside."

"Owner is one Nate Wilder." Carter had pulled up the report.

"Hang on. I know that name." Yes. The owner of Crimson Mist. I pulled up the nightclub's website again to double-check.

"Carter!" My voice rose in excitement. "Guess who owns Crimson Mist?"

"By your voice, I'm guessing Nate Wilder?"

"Yes!"

Punching Nate's name into the SIA database, my breath hitched when his mug shot appeared. Shirtless, hands on hips, he was magnificent. My fingers itched to trace the rugged outline of his well-defined abs down to the black jeans that hung low on lean hips. Curving over one shoulder and around his left arm's bicep was a tribal tattoo, thick swirls in black ink. Short brown hair casually styled as if he'd just run his fingers through it. Straight dark brows framed striking blue eyes. His nose was straight, in proportion with his cheekbones and mouth. God, what a mouth. Cupids bow above a full lower lip. And a strong jaw with just the right amount of stubble. Tapping the screen, I rotated the image. His muscled shoulders and back showed the rest of his tattoo and clear expanse of skin. He was pale, but then he was a vampire, so tanning was out of the question. But he was one mighty fine-looking vampire. Dragging my eyes from his picture, I read his file.

Vampire. 180 years old. Thirty human years at the time of turning. Retired special ops. Well, that explained his to-die-for body. Owned property in the docks, Mistlyn, and Garden District. I already knew about the warehouse at the docks and the nightclub in Mistlyn. I clicked on Garden District, and a picture of a magnificent house filled my screen. House my ass. This was a mansion. The guy must be loaded, but having been around for 180 years gave you plenty of time to accumulate a few dollars.

"We need to visit Mr. Wilder." I glanced at the time on my comms unit. Too late for tonight. The sun would be up within an hour; we'd have to sit on this until next shift.

CHAPTER
FIVE

Techno music blasted from the DJ booth, and lights flashed and swirled around the nightclub. Massive cogs of varying sizes decorated the wall behind the bar, with the bar itself lit with red strip lighting, casting eerie shadows. The place was packed, bodies squeezed together on the dance floor, the booths on the far wall full to capacity. The innovative use of scaffolding creating an upstairs balcony overlooking the main dance floor was equally packed. I pushed my way to the bar and waited to be served.

Carter was here somewhere. We'd agreed to case the joint tonight, undercover, before he took his two days leave. We'd both ditched our uniforms. Carter was sexy as sin in black jeans and T-shirt, and I was the first to admit he rocked the all-black look. I was dressed in tight black jeans and an off-the-shoulder white top that tied at my midriff. The sleeves hugged my arms to the elbow then flowed into a white lace. All in all, I exposed enough flesh without looking slutty. I hoped.

The bartender finally arrived, and I ordered vodka and cranberry juice. I ditched the straw and brought the glass to my lips, uncaring of the velvet red lipstick mark I left behind. Wanting to fit in, I'd darkened my eyes with kohl eyeliner and coated my lips with the exotic lipstick. I left my straight hair loose, and it swung around me, almost reaching my waist.

I turned my back to the bar, drink in hand, and surveyed my surroundings. Across the room, my eyes landed on Nate Wilder. He was standing with a group, talking, a tumbler of...something in his hand. I hadn't been expecting to run across him here tonight. Rumor had it that he didn't frequent the club all that often. He left the running of it to his business partner Xavier Elizondo. I continued to study him, not believing my luck. He was taller than those around him, and I felt voyeuristic as my eyes drank in his hard body. His photo didn't do him justice. In person, he was stunning.

I saw movement behind his shoulder, and my eyes landed on Carter. His dark eyes looked up and met mine. I blinked but didn't look away. He watched me for a moment before the woman at his side demanded his attention, and he turned his gaze to her. With a shuddering sigh, I gulped the rest of my drink and turned back to the bar, raising my glass to the bartender. I needed another. My body heated, and my skin tingled all over. It wasn't from the alcohol.

I was confused. What was happening? This couldn't happen with Carter. It would ruin everything. Having grown up without a mother or close girlfriends to talk to about boys, I was adrift. I wasn't a virgin, and I wasn't a prude. My body had urges, and I'd take a lover to my bed to assuage them. Never a relationship, though. One night, sometimes two, and I was done, but those encounters hadn't prepared me for the lustful thoughts I was having for my co-worker.

A pulse of energy ran along my spine, and I snapped my head up, looking into the mirror behind the bar. Carter stood behind me, not quite touching, but I could feel him, the heat of him at my back. His eyes met mine in our reflection.

"Dance with me." It wasn't a question.

I couldn't think clearly with him so close. I turned around to face him, trapped between him and the bar. I tilted my head up. So close. Dragging in a breath, I let his scent fill my nose: chocolate and musk and something else, something masculine and purely him. I still hadn't answered, just stood looking at him, praying to God I wasn't drooling. Taking my silence as consent, he took my hand and led me to the dance floor. I followed, unresisting, the electricity pulsing through me from where his hand held mine, swirling through me and pooling in my lower abdomen.

Carter pulled me into his arms loosely, leaving me room for escape if I chose. I chose not to. This was too delicious; my toes were positively curling in my boots. Our bodies moved to the heavy rhythm, and he inched closer, his hands settling on my hips. I could feel the heat of them burning through my denim jeans. Man, was it hot in here, or was it just me? The music thrummed through me, loud and primal, and I responded to the beat, letting my body bend and sway to the rhythm. I spun in his arms, pushing my back against his chest. His hands splayed across my bare abdomen, and the touch of his flesh on mine sizzled. I closed my eyes, letting my head fall back against his shoulder. I let my own hands do some exploring of their own, running down the outside of his thighs as far as I could reach, then back up again. His muscles clenched beneath my touch, and my lips curled in feminine power. A hand left my waist to brush my hair away from my shoulder, then his lips were there, nuzzling against my flesh and nibbling at my neck. My hips swayed seductively, any inhibitions long since forgotten. Carter followed my movements, his body hot against my back. He growled, his teeth grazing my skin.

He turned me in his arms, pulling me tightly against him, his hands sweeping down my back to clasp my butt and press me in closer. We barely moved, the music forgotten as we practically dry-humped each other on the dance floor. I didn't care. What I was feeling now was indescribable, and I wanted more of it.

"You smell incredible." Leaning in, he sniffed at my throat. I took in a ragged breath as he bent down and kissed the side of my neck, his teeth once again scraping my skin.

My body quivered with each touch of his mouth. I moaned when his teeth scraped, then his lips and tongue soothed. My mind was a fog. I couldn't think, just feel. With a burning need, I turned my head and sought his mouth with mine. Our lips met with a clash of teeth and tongues. I devoured him, frantic for more. I wasn't alone. He was grinding against me, his hand tangled in my hair to angle my head back for better access to my mouth. I wanted him. Wanted to feast on him until I was sated.

"Are you sure?" His voice was low and rough and brought me to my senses like a bucket of icy water being dumped on my head. Pushing away from him, I tried to get myself back under control as my heart thundered in my chest. What was that? I was curious but wary. This was a path I'd promised myself I'd never go down, yet here I was, locking lips with him and loving every second. *Jesus Christ.*

"I didn't intend for that to happen." He straightened up, making sure I had my balance before taking a step back.

"Me either," I admitted. "But I'm not sorry."

"You're not?" He looked surprised.

"That was fucking incredible." I looked him in the eye. His slight frown eased, and he grinned at me.

"It was." He ran a gentle finger down my cheek, then froze, his focus on something behind me.

"Nate Wilder is leaving the club. Let's go." He was all SIA agent. I was impressed with how quickly he switched gears: one-minute passionate wolf; the next, a cold and steely agent. It turned me on even more, and again, I was puzzled by my sudden overwhelming urge to have him. Okay, well, maybe it wasn't sudden per se, but I'd vowed never to act on it. Yet, tonight, here at the club, I was all over him like bees to honeycomb, and I wasn't feeling even the slightest twinge of remorse. Yet.

My sneakers thudded against the earth, a staccato rhythm matching my racing heart. The parklands stretched around me, an escape from the tangle with Carter earlier. I'd botched it, our years of carefully banked coals igniting in an unguarded moment. I tried to shove those embers back into darkness. Carter, ever the professional, had parted with a crisp goodnight, leaving our moment at the club unacknowledged. We'd not only run out of time, we'd lost track of Wilder. With our shift at an end and the full moon practically upon us, Carter had clocked out and headed home, leaving me with untapped energy that had my skin practically vibrating off my bones.

I pushed my pace, attempting to outrun the

persistent shadows of thought. An unexpected chill danced along my spine as a sudden symphony of birdsong broke the earlier hush. I slowed, hands bracing on my knees, breath ragged. What had jarred them into chorus? Ears straining, I heard only the crunch of gravel beneath my feet. The park's heart, once my sanctuary, now felt like a trap, dense with unseen eyes.

Pausing under the guise of a loose shoelace, I scanned the path. It lay deserted, the stillness unnerving. Not even the trees seemed to breathe. I forced my legs into a jog, each stride heavy, pushing through the cloying air.

Emerging onto the street, that prickle sharpened a silent alarm that I wasn't alone as dawn chased away the night. Each step towards HQ reminded me of my vulnerability, my holster's weight conspicuously absent. It was just me, the city, and the unsettling certainty of unseen eyes tracking my every move.

At daybreak, the first light washed the streets in a pale glow, stretching the shadows into thin, retreating silhouettes that whispered across the pavement as I walked. I could feel the cooldown beginning, the adrenaline ebbing away, replaced by a nagging restlessness that sleep wouldn't cure. The office was calling, an oasis of fluorescent lights and stale coffee—my kind of nightcap.

HQ loomed ahead, the building a silent sentinel against the early morning sky. I opened the door, stepping into the familiar buzz of late-night casework. It was a relief, in a way. With Carter gone for his lunar hiatus, the air was lighter, easier to breathe. Wolves are pack animals, and Carter was no exception. Twice a month, he would vanish into the night—once for the transformation and once to recover from its toll. I often wondered what secrets he chased under the glow of the full moon, what wild freedom he found there that eluded him in his human shackles.

The sense of being watched dissipated the closer I got to HQ. It clicked then—someone had been tailing me, slipping through the shadows since the club. My gut twisted at the thought.

Once inside, I breezed through security with a press of my thumb and shot down to the fourth floor. The change rooms offered a quick respite, the hot water sluicing away the park's grime and the last remnants of unease. Back in uniform, I settled into the familiar groove of my desk, the virtual case board flickering to life under my gaze.

A prompt flashed, nudging me to ring the

morgue. I flicked on the comms unit, my wrist buzzing to life.

"Remember how I said I'd try and see if the other victims had that stamp, or traces of a stamp, from that nightclub?" The tech's voice spilled out, a notch too high, betraying his excitement.

"Sure. How did it go?"

"Well, I couldn't pull a complete stamp, but there are traces of the same type of ink used. I mean, the stamp could have come from any establishment that uses fluorescent ink. I can't prove it came from the same nightclub."

"It's a start. I'll see if I can get video surveillance from Crimson Mist around the time all the victims disappeared. A day or two before the time of death would be the timeframe we're looking for then, right?"

"Yeah, I'd imagine so. The ink doesn't last more than forty-eight hours, so to pull a trace, they had to have been stamped anytime within the two days prior to death."

With a thank you, I cut the connection, my mind already sifting through the next steps. I couldn't afford to sit on this. I needed to move. Time wasted could mean life or death for another potential victim. I punched in Nate Wilder's number.

"Wilder," he said, no preamble. The man answered his own calls; color me surprised.

"Enforcer Black with the SIA. Mr. Wilder, I presume?"

"That's me. What can I do for you, Enforcer Black?" Curiosity laced his words, a thread of intrigue.

"I need a bit of your time to discuss an ongoing investigation. I'd be happy to meet with you wherever is convenient, or you are most welcome to attend the SIA offices."

He paused. "Can I ask what this is regarding?"

"Four human murders."

"And I'm a suspect?"

"Not necessarily. But I do have some questions."

"Fine. I'm free now. Come to my home. I prefer not to travel under sunlight."

"Of course. I'll see you shortly."

The Garden District was more than beautiful; it was a canvas of history, each house a brushstroke of luxury and legacy. I halted at the gates of Nate Wilder's mansion, a structure that whispered wealth in its silent, stone-clad stature. After announcing my arrival through the intercom, the gates opened, welcoming me onto the property.

The drive up to the house was a sensory journey. Shafts of sunlight pierced the canopy of willow branches, sketching a mosaic of light and shadow upon the mansion's facade. The air was heavy with the sweet perfume of jasmine, an invisible cloud that wrapped around me, seeping into my clothes and hair. The crunch of gravel under my tires punctuated the quiet as I made my approach.

Before me stood a Victorian mansion, its white columns, and ironwork balconies meticulously restored, a nod to a gilded age. I parked and stepped onto the circular driveway, a subtle thrill of nervousness accompanying me as I walked up the steps to the grand entrance, ready to cross the threshold into Nate Wilder's world.

The door swung open, and a maid, young and poised, welcomed me with a practiced smile. She stepped aside, and I entered, momentarily lost for words. The grandeur of the entrance hall was a spectacle, twin staircases sweeping up, reaching for a grand balcony above.

The floor—a canvas of tiles—spun the tale of an ancient tree, its branches sprawling across the cool stone, inviting the eye to wander and the mind to marvel. I'd imagine the design looked stunning from the balcony.

Guided into an adjoining parlor, the air seemed to pulse with an unseen presence.

"Mr. Wilder? Your guest," the maid announced, her voice soft yet clear in the vastness of the opulent space.

With a gentle click, the door closed, and I found

myself alone with him. He set aside a magazine upon my entrance, rising to meet me, his presence commanding the room.

"Ah," he murmured, moving toward me. "Enforcer Black, I assume?"

"Thank you for agreeing to meet with me on such short notice."

"Pleasure." The way he drawled the word had me thinking of what I'd done with Carter the night before. My thighs clenched.

I sighed, pulling the zip of my Kevlar jacket down ever so slightly so it wasn't so constrictive around my tight throat. I moved across to the windows. It was daylight outside, yet the sun wasn't bothering him. I assumed it had a special UV tint, reaching out and pressing my palm against the window, the coolness of it soothing.

He resumed his seat, leaning back, a picture of casual authority, legs stretched out, arms draped with effortless power. "Go ahead," he said, his voice slicing through the tension like a blade.

I gathered my thoughts, feeling the weight of his gaze. "Four victims," I began, "one with your club's stamp on her hand, found in *your* warehouse. The others, similar marks, but the details are murky."

His response was immediate, a sharpened edge

to his certainty. "Let's get one thing straight—I've defended this country, put my life on the line. Hurting someone? That's not in my playbook. Secondly, I haven't been to that warehouse since I bought it nine or ten years ago."

I found myself nodding, wanting to trust his conviction. "The warehouse," I pressed on, "you haven't set foot in it for almost a decade?"

"A politician's promise gone sour," he dismissed with a flick of his wrist. "Thought it'd turn into my next club. Turned out to be a bust."

"Why hold on to it?" I probed, curiosity piqued.

He unfolded his arms, sitting forward. "Let's just say I'm not one to throw away a potential opportunity. If the right buyer comes along, sure, I'll sell. But for now, it sits."

"The victim had your nightclub stamp on her hand." I ventured.

A ghost of a smile touched his lips. "I might just be able to help you with that."

"How?"

"We have security cameras everywhere. We can go through the footage and see if your victims did visit the club. And who they left with."

The suggestion hovered between us; his offer dangled like a perfectly baited hook. My lips curved into a smile, silently acknowledging his proactive move. He reclined, his eyes never leaving mine, a silent observer gauging my reaction.

"One term," he stipulated, his voice measured, a calm before the inevitable storm.

I arched an eyebrow. "Which is?"

He matched my posture, leaning in. "I'm in this with you," he declared. My instinct was to refuse, to maintain that professional boundary, but he cut through my resistance with a rationale as sharp as cut glass. "If my club is the stage for this macabre play and I'm being cast as the villain, it's only right I get a role in rewriting the script." There was no mistaking the resolve in his tone nor the undercurrent of a threat if crossed.

"That's not my decision to make. Above my pay grade. You'll need to talk to Director Ridgeway. And she's off until tomorrow. Full moon and all."

"Your director is a werewolf?"

"Affirmative. The SIA has all sorts of supernaturals and paranormals."

"What are you? You're not vampire or werewolf." I saw him raise his nose slightly and sniff my scent.

"No, I'm not either of those things." I agreed. "Let's not get off track. I need to get moving on this case before we have another victim on our hands.

Where can I view the footage?" I was prepared to beg. He had what I needed to move forward in catching whoever was behind the human hunts.

"I have an IT lab here. My team and I occasionally freelance…as private investigators."

"Really? I didn't know that, but okay." I nodded; an IT lab indeed. This could be the big breakthrough I needed.

"Doesn't pay to advertise the fact. Civilians can often gain much more useful intel than any agency." Standing, he strode across the room, beckoning me to follow.

He led me through the massive house to a staircase cleverly concealed at the rear of the property. As we descended the stairs, the transformation from the luxurious to the secretive was palpable. The bunker's entrance greeted us with a heavy steel door, which swung open at the sound of his voice, revealing a stark contrast to the mansion's opulence. Inside, a high-tech command center was segmented into four distinct areas by glass walls—each with its own story to tell.

To the right, a surveillance hub buzzed with activity, screens aglow with the silent watch over unseen places. Opposite, a medical bay stood ready, its gurneys and cabinets a silent testament to emergencies and careful planning. The air was alive with the low hum of state-of-the-art systems, the kind you don't find in civilian life.

Down the central pathway, scientific inquiry had its domain, with microscopes and apparatus neatly arrayed for tasks unknown. And at the end, the sight of holding cells—sterile and empty—echoed with the possibility of what they might contain. It was a space that spoke of preparation and power, a place that balanced the fine line between sanctuary and interrogation, leaving me with a sense of respect tinged with a ripple of trepidation.

"Wow. Quite the setup," I murmured, impressed.

Nate guided me into the computer lab, the glass door sliding closed behind us silently.

"Can I log into the SIA server from here?"

"Sure." He indicated a monitor along the far wall. I pulled out the chair beneath it and laid my hands across the thin membrane keyboard, keying in the SIA server's address and my login credentials. I'd just gained access when the door behind us slid open. I glanced over my shoulder at the newcomer.

Another tall one, though his build was leaner than Nate's. His hair hung in waves to his shoulders, a light brown color that matched the light beard he sported. His hazel eyes met mine.

"Ethan, meet Enforcer Black. We are assisting the SIA with their inquiries surrounding Crimson Mist."

I rose and extended my hand to the other man. "Please, go ahead and call me Raven."

"Raven Black?" Nate looked at me.

"The nuns chose the name Raven, and a social worker chose my surname. I suppose they thought they were funny." I shrugged.

"Pleased to meet you, Raven." Ethan shook my hand and then moved over to the main terminal in the center of the room. "So what are we doing?"

"I'm after footage from the club, seeing if we can spot any of my four victims. We know one of them was at Crimson Mist, so I want to check out who she was with and if anything happened while she was there. We don't know if the others were at Crimson Mist, but if they were at a club, then Crimson Mist might be the clue linking our victims together. I'm just pulling up pictures and dates now." I returned to my computer and pulled up the victim's ID photos, taking care the vampires didn't get a glimpse of the morgue shots.

"I've been playing with a 3D facial recognition

software," Ethan told me, "I'll give it a run first, might save us some time."

I sent him the files and then sat back and watched as his hands flew across his touchscreen setup. Touching, grabbing, swiping. Manipulating files with his fingers. He loaded up Allena Niles's image and ran the app. The video played in fast forward, tracking, measuring, and discarding faces and pictures. We'd been at it for half an hour when the video froze, and a face outlined in red zeroed in on the screen.

"Got her." Ethan grinned. He moved the video frame by frame as Allena shuffled forward in the lineup outside the club, made it to the front, and received the stamp on the back of her hand. The footage was date-stamped three days ago. The search resumed, picking up bits of footage from inside the club. At the bar buying a drink. Dancing. She appeared to be there with girlfriends, and they all left together. Everything looked fine. So she wasn't taken from the club. Ethan copied the footage we needed, loaded up the first victim's image, and set the date range I gave him. Hours passed as we trawled through the recordings. We'd found the second victim, she'd been at the club as suspected, but again, nothing untoward happened there.

I rubbed my eyes and yawned. I'd been up all night and, glancing at the time on my phone, half the day. If I could get all the footage I needed before starting my next shift, I could begin cross-referencing and identify if the victims interacted with the same person or had the same group of friends. It was a big job, but it was the only lead we had. I propped my elbow on the desk and rested my head against my palm, tired eyes watching the video stream. I could hear Ethan and Nate talking, their voices becoming muted as my eyes closed.

With a jerk, I opened my eyes. My comms unit was buzzing. I reached for my wrist, confused to discover I was lying down. *Where was I?* A scraping noise reached my ears, and I froze. Not knowing where I was and what was happening, I pulsed out my power. I heard a muffled oath and quickly sat up, reaching for my pyre gun, only to find it missing.

"It's okay. You're safe." Nate's voice. I rubbed at my eyes, scanning the room. I was on one of the gurneys in the first aid room. And there was my gun on the trolley by my side. My eyes met Nate's as he stood frozen. We were in the bunker. *Right, right, I remembered now.* Releasing him, I pulled my power back in.

My fingers fumbled for a brief second, betraying a flicker of unease as I pressed the button on my comms unit, the silent reproach for my tardiness clear in the flashing light. The SIA's protocol for missed shifts was non-negotiable—a security check to account for the whereabouts of their agents. I had let the enigma of Nate Wilder's world ensnare me, a misstep I rarely made.

"Agent Black," I spoke into the device, my tone steady despite the slight quickening of my pulse. "Confirming my status: I'm secure. Got held up, but I'll be at headquarters shortly."

A pause hung on the other end, long enough for me to feel the scrutiny from afar.

"Copy that. Ensure your immediate check-in upon arrival. Stay sharp and stay safe."

I lowered my arm, aware of Nate's gaze on me, his curiosity piqued not so much by the interruption but by my reaction to being jerked awake. "Sorry about that," I mumbled.

"That was unexpected." Nate approached warily, hands out, indicating he meant no harm.

"I bet. Sorry again. I was disorientated. I don't remember falling asleep." Picking up one of my discarded boots from the floor, he eased my foot into it, slowly drawing the zip up the inside of my calf.

"You ran out of steam a couple of hours ago. Figured you'd be more comfortable in here rather than face down on the desk."

"I didn't drool, did I?"

"No, but you did snore."

I snorted. "Did not!" I paused. "Did I?"

He laughed, pulling on my other boot and lifting me from the gurney. "Nah. Now tell me, what was that little stunt?"

"Yeah, the old chill-and-halt trick," I quipped with an offhand shrug, making light of the ability that so often put me under the microscope. "It's just a part of the package, no explanation included. Fascinating, right?" As his mouth opened, likely to dive into the usual barrage of questions, I raised a palm. "Hold that thought. Human anatomy still calls the shots, and right now, it's calling for a bathroom break."

His face was etched with intrigue, clearly itching to dissect the enigma of my power, but my pressing need would have to take precedence over his curiosity.

"Topside for bathrooms," he announced. "And I'm betting you're starved." My stomach backed his bet with a well-timed grumble. I shot it a glare—it had the worst timing. He caught my hand, a spark of warmth in his touch, and we were heading back upstairs before I could protest. He left me at the bathroom door, a finger pointing down the hall, indicating the kitchen.

Inside, I faced the mirror. The woman staring back boasted panda eyes—a true indication of my severe lack of sleep. With a splash of water, I tried to erase the evidence, running my fingers through my hair to restore order. "Three hours of shut-eye is a new personal best," I muttered to my reflection, sarcastic as ever. Leaving the bathroom, I hurried down the hallway to the kitchen, finding Nate looking decidedly sheepish.

"I'm sorry. We don't have much...food...in the house." He was looking at the fridge, and my curiosity got the better of me. I opened it. Inside, stacked neatly shelf upon shelf, were bags of blood.

"Okay then." I closed the door and glanced around the kitchen. Designer. Top of the range.

"I'll order something in. Pizza? Chinese?" He suggested.

"No, please, I need to head to work anyway. I'll grab something on the way. I hadn't meant to be here so long. Sorry for the imposition."

"I liked having you here." He sounded surprised. The thing is, I liked being here with him and Ethan as well. They were easy company, and Ethan was an IT genius. The footage he'd found was invaluable to the investigation.

"We need to talk," Nate said.

I turned to look at him. "Talk?"

"The investigation. It's obvious the connection you're looking for is Crimson Mist. Anything to do with my club, I will be involved in."

"I'm not saying no, Nate. It's not up to me. Like I said, you'll have to take it up with the director."

"Who's off being a wolf tonight."

"You're not species prejudice, are you, Nate?"

"Of course not! If you knew me better, you'd never suggest that."

"But I don't know you better. And you're pushing me on something I have no control over." I puffed out a frustrated breath. Lord, I was tired, and I didn't want to argue with him. "I've got to go." Pulling myself together, I turned, walking away without looking back.

EIGHT

"Better start talking, Miller. I don't have all day." Leaning my elbows on the steel table, I watched the agitated werewolf across from me. His hands were in chains, silver, and cuffed to the table, and around his neck was a thick glowing collar. The collar emitted a frequency directly into the wearer's skin that stopped them from transforming. And given that it was now the full moon, Miller needed to change. And soon.

Miller was the wolf we'd picked up a couple of days ago who'd alluded to human hunts. There was no way this drop kick was behind organizing anything, but keeping him on ice until the full moon gave me leverage to get more information from him.

"What ya wanna know?" he snapped. His skin was covered in sweat, his hair damp with it. He badly needed to shift.

"The humans you were hunting in Wolf's Hill. How did that come about?"

"Just stumbled across them. Campers."

"You're lying." I rose to my feet, getting ready to leave.

"Wait, wait!" he pleaded, desperate. "I'll tell ya."

I sat back down. "Fuck me around again, and I will rip your kidney out, fill it with nails and feed it back to you. Understand?"

He nodded. "Ma'am."

"And don't fucking call me ma'am," I snapped. I was tired, hungry, and out of patience.

"We bought the humans," he muttered, head bowed.

"Where?"

"An auction."

"When?"

"The same day you caught us."

"Where was this auction held?" I pressed.

"House way out back of Mistlyn."

"What house? Do you have an address? Have you been there before?"

"Can't remember the address. They move them around. Never told the location until the day of the auction."

"Who organizes it?"

"Don't know."

"Who. Organizes. It." He had to know. Otherwise, how would he purchase his produce?

"I don't know. Honestly. We deal with just one guy, Brooks, who texts us the location. But only if we're planning on going. Brooks has his own group of buyers, and we don't see who else is there, just what's on offer to buy."

"How often are these auctions held?"

"Every few weeks."

"And you go to all of them?"

"No. Just when we're planning on some fun."

"Ah, yes. Let's talk about your fun. So you bought your humans this week. Why?"

He looked puzzled. "Like I told ya. Fun."

"Why buy them this week? Because of the full moon? You planning to let your wolves eat them?"

He shrugged, which I took as a yes.

"So why did we catch you chasing them? Why not keep them safe and sound until tonight?"

"To give 'em a taste of what's coming, make

them nice and desperate. We keep 'em in a cave in the forest, and when we're ready for the hunt, they're half crazy and fight more. Make better prey."

"You sick fuck." I looked at the sorry excuse for a wolf in front of me. I wanted to terminate his pathetic existence, but unfortunately, it was against SIA policy.

"These auctions, they just for werewolves?" I asked.

"Shit, no. Anyone can buy, even other humans."

"What? Why would a human want to buy another human?"

"Usually only the filthy rich and s'far as I heard, they buy 'em for sex. Keep 'em locked up and do the weird kinky shit they don't want no one knowing about."

"Vampires as well?"

"Course! They buy 'em for blood slaves and sex, too, I guess, though vamps don't need no sex slaves. But you got those that refuse bagged blood and only drink from the vein but want it on tap."

Where there was demand, someone would always find a way to supply. Sitting back with a sigh, I rubbed my hands over my face. This was so fucked up.

"I want a picture of this guy, Brooks."

"I don't have no pictures."

"Then you'll work with our graphics guy until we get a digital composite of what Brooks looks like."

"What?"

"A sketch artist. Once we have a sketch of this guy, Brooks, then I'll take that collar off."

I left the interrogation room, stopping to arrange for the graphics officer to visit. I'd keep my word and allow Miller's collar to be removed, but he'd be confined to his cell. I badly wanted to terminate the little shit, but he could have more useful information. I'd ask Carter to have a crack at him when he returned to work.

Back at my desk, I brought up my holovision screen. A message from the Medical Lab was waiting for me.

"Enforcer Black - as per Director Ridgeway's policy regarding security clearance for any SIA agents who carry human DNA, you are required to undergo quarterly medical examinations. You have been scheduled to undergo testing at three a.m. Please be on time."

What the? I punched the medical unit's number

into my comms. I'd never heard of any such policy, and I sure as hell wasn't going to consent to the continual prodding, poking, and invasiveness of their testing on a regular basis. I'd been subjected to more than enough of that by the humans.

"Medical."

"This is Enforcer Black. I received your communication that I'm to report for a medical exam today. Care to explain to me what the hell that is all about?"

"As the memo states, the director has requested it."

"Why is this the first I'm hearing of it?"

"She implemented the new policy last night. We simply follow the directives we're given."

"And who else, besides me, will be having these medicals?"

"You are the only agent who is affected."

Just as I thought. "This is bullshit." I fumed. Always being singled out because I was different. I didn't fit into the human world, and I didn't fit into the supernatural one either.

"We expect you here at three a.m., Enforcer." He hung up. Urgh. I stormed to the recs room and made myself a coffee. The clock on the wall indicated it had just passed two. With this whole medical shit tossed into my night, there was no way I'd get back out into the field tonight. Plus, I was exhausted; I could barely see straight. After my medical, I was clocking out and catching up on some sleep.

Stepping out of the elevator the following evening, I was relieved Carter looked refreshed and relaxed at his desk. I'd slept for ten hours by the time I'd gotten home at daybreak. I'd been running on below empty when I'd finally stumbled through my front door. The medical was as horrendous as I'd been expecting. Multiple blood samples, ultrasounds, x-rays, an internal exam, even a spinal tap that left me with a thumping headache and feeling like an overused and under-loved pin cushion. I didn't understand why I'd been singled out, but I'd be taking it up with the director.

"You look like you could use some R and R,"

Carter commented as I sank into my chair. "You're paler than usual."

"Geez, don't start. You've been back, what, five minutes, and already you're nagging."

"No, seriously, Raven. I'm not kidding. You look like shit. What happened while I was away?"

"I look like shit—thanks for that, by the way—because the director has implemented a new policy for unassigned paranormals. We're to undergo medical testing every three months."

"Testing? As in?"

"Nasty, invasive, painful."

"Well, shit."

"Exactly. They took a shit ton of blood yesterday, not to mention spinal fluid, which has left me feeling—and looking—like crap."

"I'm going to talk to the director. That's bullshit."

"Cool it, wolf boy. I can fight my own battles, and I'll be speaking with her myself. This doesn't concern you."

"It concerns me if it's about you."

"No. It doesn't. I'm not your concern, Carter, and what happened at the nightclub shouldn't have happened. Now can we please just focus on this case?"

I could feel his gaze boring into me, but I refused to look up from my screen. I didn't have the energy to argue with him today. Heaving a dramatic sigh, Carter gave in.

"I see you got your hands on Crimson Mist footage," he said, changing the subject.

"I did. They were very helpful." Ethan had given me the footage I needed, and I'd uploaded it to our case file on the SIA server.

"So we've got all four victims at the nightclub."

"Yes. But they weren't taken from the club. We just know that they were all there prior to their abduction. Now that you're back, I think searching the nightclub could be beneficial."

"Exactly what I was thinking. I'll draw up the warrant. Pretty sure Ridgeway will authorize it."

Cradling my second coffee, I let the caffeine work its magic, clearing the fog from my mind. I listened to Carter typing up the warrant, my mind drifting to yesterday and the medical procedures I'd endured. The more I thought about them, the angrier I got. I had to take action on this. *Now*.

Riding the elevator to the director's floor, I imagined different scenarios as to why she had ordered the barrage of tests and why they had to be an ongoing thing. What had changed? No one had cared that I was an unclassified paranormal. Why all the fuss now?

The director's assistant rushed after me as I strode past her desk without pausing.

"You can't see the director without an appointment, Agent." Her voice rose several octaves as she tried to block me from entering the director's office.

"It'll only take a minute." I cupped her shoulders and firmly moved her to the side, opened the door, and stepped inside. The director's office was the epitome of modern luxury. Glass table, fur rug on the floor, leather sofa off to one side, and a glass coffee table that matched her desk. The director sighed when she saw me.

"Black. To what do I owe this pleasure?" Her red lips twisted in a mockery of a smile, her short red bob swinging as she tilted her head. She was an attractive woman, but cold...as cold as ice.

"I want to know why you ordered the medical assessment on me."

"Not just you, Black. All unclassified paranormals."

"And we both know I'm the only unclassified paranormal here, so cut the bullshit."

"Direct as ever." She rose, smoothing the crisp

white shirt she wore over her hips. Director Kelli Ridgeway was always impeccably dressed, and today was no different. Smart black slacks, white silk shirt, red stilettoes, perfectly made-up face.

"There are murmurings from the Council that they are considering changing the entry requirements into the SIA, that only classifieds will be permitted. I'm trying to get ahead of the game and have you classified, so it becomes a moot point for us."

"The Council is behind this? Why are they even bothered with what we're doing, so long as we're getting rogues off the streets?"

She shrugged, walking around to the front of her desk and leaning against it.

"Who knows? And it's not official. Yet. And if they end up dropping it, fine, but it can't hurt to find out what you are in the meantime."

"News flash. *It hurts*. It hurts me. Are an internal examination and a spinal tap necessary? What do my vagina and cervix have to do with anything?"

"I admit that sounds extreme. I'll have the medical team desist from such invasive procedures in the future. Now that we have those results, they will have to find other methods to identify you." She focused her gaze somewhere beyond my left shoulder.

"We?" I pounced.

"What?" Her gaze bounced back to me, frowning.

"You said '*we*' have those results. What did you mean?"

A flush of red crept up the director's neck and bloomed across her cheeks. Her eyes flashed. She was angry. I wondered why. Because I was questioning her? Or calling her out on her bullshit. I wasn't convinced the Council was behind this, but if not them, then who?

"*We* as in the SIA. Now, you'll have to excuse me, Black. If you want that warrant for Crimson Mist authorized, I suggest you leave my office. Now." Her voice was cold, hardened steel. Oh yeah, she was pissed at me.

It was early in clubbing standards when we dropped into Crimson Mist, warrant in hand. Nate wasn't there, but the nightclub's manager, Xavier Elizondo, was. Xavier sported an impressive head of hair, long and multicolored, that passed his shoulders in a shaggy cut that seemed to have a life of its own. He was dressed in skin-tight leather pants and a leather vest, undone, revealing a hair-free chest and nipple ring. That wasn't his only piercing. He had a bar through his eyebrow, a nose ring, and two lip piercings.

"Nate told me you'd probably be dropping by." Xavier had a voice as smooth as honey, and I bet he used it to win the ladies and maybe the men, too, judging by how he was eyeing Carter up and down.

"Did he, now?" I drew his attention back to me. "Then you won't mind at all if we have a look around."

"By all means!" Xavier extended his arms in an exaggerated gesture.

"We'll start with your office. Or Mr. Wilder's, if he has one here."

"Mr. Wilder? So formal." Xavier snickered. "He doesn't spend much time here, so we share an office. This way."

We followed Xavier through a doorway and into a corridor. I heard Carter's sharp intake of breath and knew he was picking up on smells I'd never be able to detect. Ignoring him, I hurried down the spiral staircase to the floor below. Xavier led us down a long hallway, the crimson carpet silencing our footsteps. The walls had been papered with a black and silver design, and dim wall sconces cast just enough light to see by. We passed a dozen closed doors before reaching the double doors at the end.

"What's in all these rooms?" I asked.

"Feeding rooms. Take a look." Xavier opened the door closest to us. The room was small, decorated with the same carpet and wall coverings as the hallway. Inside was a black sofa, at the end of that, a small cupboard.

"What's in the cupboard?"

"Towels. Tissues. Cleaning items." Xavier shrugged.

Carter had backed away from the open door, and by the disgust on his face, I'm guessing he was getting a nose full of stale scents.

Xavier led us into his office, leaving the doors open behind him. His and Nate's office did not disappoint. The room was huge, with plush crimson carpet beneath our feet, black leather armchairs, a sofa in the center of the room, a massive black desk with a huge red swivel chair behind it. An identical setup occupied the other side of the room, almost a mirror image if not for the different items on the desk and in the bookshelves behind each desk.

"My desk." Xavier pointed to the left. "And Nate's." Indicating the right. At the far end of the office was a row of black filing cabinets, all identical.

"Thank you." Carter stepped forward, arm outstretched to indicate the sofa in the middle of the room. "Please take a seat while we begin. Black, you take Mr. Elizondo's desk, and I'll do Wilder's."

He'd called me Black. Carter only did that when

he was annoyed. I watched his rigid back for a minute before sighing and getting to work. We were minutes into the search when Carter pulled out a pink mobile phone from the top drawer of Nate's desk.

"Care to explain this?" he asked Xavier, brows raised. "I find it hard to believe that a man like Nate Wilder has a pink cell phone."

"That's not Nate's." Xavier shrugged.

"Whose is it then?"

"No idea."

"Someone leave it at the club, perhaps?"

"Lost and found is kept at the bar, not here."

Carter pressed a few buttons on the phone and swore under his breath. "Holy Shit. Check this out."

I hurried over to his side, and he held the phone out to me. He'd pulled up a picture of our fourth victim, smiling into the camera with the packed dance floor of the club behind her. She'd snapped a selfie while she was here.

"It's Allena Niles's phone," Carter said.

"What's it doing here?"

"Perhaps he forgot to get rid of it."

"This seems too easy," I said. "If Nate's behind this, he wouldn't leave a victim's phone in such an easy-to-find place. He'd be smart enough to get rid of it, or if he did need it for something, he'd hide it away in a secure spot, not chuck it in the top drawer of his desk."

"The chick's right," Xavier chimed in. "Nate's had military training. He's no fool. That's been planted."

"I tend to agree." I nodded.

"Sure you have an unbiased view?" Carter's gaze was cold and hard. I hated it when he was angry with me.

"It isn't what you think, Alex."

"You're calling me Alex. This can't be good. So you slept with him."

"No. I didn't."

"Something happened."

"Nothing happened. Not that I have to answer to you. Bag the phone, and let's keep searching." I didn't know what tipped Carter off. I could only assume he'd picked up the mixture of my scent and Nate's. If Nate had visited the club after my visit to his home, my scent would have been all over him.

Carter held my gaze for a moment longer before nodding and turning away. Our search continued for several hours, and the club was jumping by the time we finished, but we'd failed to turn up anything else.

"About the other night." Carter waited until we were in the SUV and heading back to HQ.

"No." I really didn't want to talk about it.

"I know we've always had this unspoken 'thing' and that we'd agreed we wouldn't cross that line, which makes what happened a bit more...strange."

"What do you mean?" I frowned. What was he getting at?

"It felt out of control, didn't it?" he asked. I nodded. Yes, it had felt totally out of control. And out of the blue. And I was too scared to think about it in case I wanted it again.

"So, during the search at the nightclub, I discovered something."

"Oh?"

"They pump pheromones into the club."

"They what?"

"Found canisters in the basement with tubes hooking up to the air-conditioning system."

"So we were...under the influence?"

"They heighten what's already there. It's not like they're mind-altering drugs, but it does explain why we wanted to inexplicably jump each other's bones."

"Oh." I didn't know what to say. At the time, I'd been prepared to strip him naked and ride him like a cowgirl, consequences be damned. But later, when reality kicked in, or more likely when the pheromones wore off, I'd been full of regret, cursing myself for almost ruining our friendship.

"It's okay, Raven. We're good." He reached out and patted my thigh, his palm burning hot through the fabric of my pants. *Yeah, right.*

As soon as we were back at HQ, Carter logged the phone into evidence, turning it over to the IT guys and forensics to do their thing. I'd barely settled into my seat when my comms unit buzzed. It was the director.

"Black."

"I've just issued the order to have Wilder brought in for questioning. See that it's done."

"Not a problem." But she'd disconnected the call. I opened my mouth to tell Carter we had to head out again when the order appeared on our screens.

"Geez, that was quick," Carter muttered, pushing to his feet.

"A record," I agreed. "That was the director on

my comms unit issuing the order. She's all over this one."

"Maybe she's getting fallout from the Council?"

"Could be. She's blaming them for the sudden interest in determining what I am."

"Seriously? Why would the Council care? As long as you're doing your job and getting results?"

"Well, if they classify me as human, I'll be fired. I wonder if the Police would take me if I'm sacked from the SIA? The irony is that I was sacked from the SIA because I'm not paranormal, unable to work for the Police because they consider me paranormal."

"It won't come to that. The director is in your corner on this one. That's why she's pushing hard to get you classified."

I was silent. I wasn't sure I believed the Council was interested in my classification at all. I suspected the director was using them as a shield, hiding behind their power to order the testing, but I had no proof, just a hunch, and until I had something to back me up, I was keeping it to myself.

"You think Wilder is involved?" Carter asked on the way out to the Garden District.

"Actually, no, I don't. The guy's former military. He's smart. If he wanted to kidnap humans for some reason, well, for starters, he wouldn't take them from his own club. Second, he'd find a way to make sure their bodies were never found. And finally, he wouldn't keep items belonging to his victims. And especially at the club. It's all too clumsy."

"Agreed. I wonder why the director was so quick to issue the order?"

"Protocol. Doesn't matter what we think. Protocol dictates he be brought in for formal questioning. Plus, none of the evidence with the first three victims ties him to them, just the last one. Allena. Her body was found in his warehouse. His club stamp on her hand. Her phone in his desk."

"The other victims did have his stamp, though," Carter pointed out.

"Possibly. The stamp wasn't clearly identifiable as Crimson Mist on the other victims. All we know is that the same ink was used. And it wasn't until we started digging and found the footage that we linked them together."

"Almost like someone was using Allena's death as breadcrumbs. To lead us to Wilder."

"Seems that way. I think we need to be looking into Wilder's enemies. Who would benefit if he was put away for this? One of his staff or friends? Or someone outside the circle? A competitor? And that still doesn't answer our question of what's happening to these people. Why are they mutating?"

We pulled up outside Nate's house. I let Carter take the lead, standing back when he pounded on the front door. The same young woman who'd greeted me earlier opened the door, recognizing me with a smile.

"Agent." She nodded her head at me, then turned her attention to Carter. "Yes? How can I help you?"

"We need to talk to Nate Wilder. Official SIA business." Carter tapped his fingers on the red badge on his belt.

"I'm sorry, Agent, Mr. Wilder is not in residence."

"Not in residence? What does that even mean?" Carter asked.

"He's not at home. Have you tried his club, Crimson Mist?"

"We were at his club a couple of hours ago. He wasn't there. When did he leave here?"

"He has been out all evening."

"And you don't know where he went?"

"I'm his employee, Agent. He doesn't report his business to me."

"Could you take a guess as to where he might be?"

"I'm sorry, I don't know." With that, she very gently closed the door in our faces.

"We could search the place," Carter muttered, facing me.

"I don't think he's here. We'd just be wasting our time. Let's recheck the club. Maybe he turned up after we left."

He wasn't at the club. We tried a few other venues we thought a millionaire vampire might frequent, but we were out of luck. It appeared Nate Wilder had gone to ground. The director wouldn't be happy.

ELEVEN

As soon as my shift was over, I changed into my running gear and took to the park, blowing out my frustration and the chewing out the director had given us when we'd failed to return with Nate. I wasn't long into my jog when I had the same sensation as before. I was being watched; I was sure of it. Again, I did the shoelace trick, crouching and glancing around, and again I came up with nothing, yet the hairs on the back of my neck still stood at attention.

Rather than pushing myself hard, which had been my intention, I slowed my pace to a steady jog, leaving myself some extra energy should anyone be foolish enough to try and jump me. My ponytail bounced across my back with each step, my breath coming in and out in a steady rhythm, belying my anxiety. So much for a relaxing workout.

The next thing, I was face down on the ground, a heavy weight on top of me, my wrists expertly pinned and held in the middle of my back with just enough pressure for me to know if I wriggled, it would hurt. I kept still, tried to flex my fingers to throw my power out and freeze this son of a bitch, but I was powerless. My power came from my hands. If they were incapacitated, so was I. Some clever bastard had worked that out.

"What do you want?" My voice sounded like rusty nails, partly pain, partly temper.

"I'm not going to hurt you. I just need you to listen." The hot breath at my ear had my body tensing in realization.

"Nate, you absolute idiot. What the hell are you doing?"

"I know you want to bring me in. I just need more time." He slipped restraints around my wrists and pulled tight, then eased his weight off of me and jerked me into a sitting position, facing him. Dressed in black jeans and a black hoodie, he was darkly thrilling and up there with the sexiest men on the planet.

"You're making a big mistake doing this."

"I'm not guilty. I didn't hurt those people."

"I know you didn't. But this isn't how you go about proving your innocence. This is only going to make things worse for you."

He shrugged. "The director denied my request to be involved in the investigation. Said I was a suspect. I can't have that."

"So you decided to go all vigilante to prove a point?"

"Not prove a point. To prove I'm not involved, not responsible. And if I can't do that via the SIA, then I'll do it by any means necessary."

"Attacking me is any means necessary?"

"Not attacking. Just temporarily subduing your powers so you can't freeze me."

"Why me?"

"Because I have no desire to do this to Agent Carter!" Before I could ask what he meant, he leaned forward and planted his lips on mine. It was...nice. He was skilled; he'd undoubtedly had plenty of practice, but he didn't flip my switch the way Carter did. I cursed myself for the comparison. Carter was off-limits—he wasn't, and never could be, mine.

Slowly Nate pulled back, chuckling a little. "Not doing it for you, huh?"

"I'm not a restraints type of girl."

His gray eyes had darkened, flashing black with desire. Okay, so ties and handcuffs and other such things were his jam.

"I'm sorry." His voice was low on the night air.

"You should be. This isn't the answer. Tying me up or kissing me."

"A miscalculation on my part." I got the feeling no one turned down this guy's kisses, and judging by the look on his face, he was genuinely puzzled at my response.

"Let me go," I demanded, pulling against my ties.

"Soon. But I need to fix this first."

"No, you don't. Let me take you in. Just for questioning, Nate, just a formality. We don't think you're guilty, the evidence is circumstantial, but we still need to bring you in."

"No. *I* will clear my name."

"You're making this worse, I swear. If you don't come in, the director could issue an arrest warrant. Then it will be even harder to sort this mess out."

"I'm sorry," he said again, dropping one last kiss on my lips, and he was gone. I sighed. Damn foolish vampire. I wasn't sure how much was male pride and how much was a vampire thing, but either way, he was going about clearing his name all wrong.

I knew I should report him for this. Attacking an SIA agent, off duty or not, was a serious offense. Mulling over my options, which were all of two, I pulled my bound hands under my butt, wriggled until they were under my legs, and finally maneuvered until I'd pulled my legs through the loop of my arms. My hands were now bound in front of me. He'd used standard plastic cable ties. Strong, but easy to break if you know how. Raising my hands above my head, I brought them down sharply against my upturned knee. The plastic snapped with a sting to my flesh. Picking up the broken tie and shoving it in my pocket, I headed home, too wound up to finish my run.

I didn't care to examine my plan not to turn in this little stunt of Nate's to the SIA. Not reporting him could mean my badge, but the minute I shoved the plastic restraints into my pockets, I'd subconsciously decided not to report him or the incident. I had to be crazy. I briefly considered calling Carter and asking him to use his wolf senses to track Nate, but again, I did nothing. Nothing more than return to my car at the SIA and drive home.

As dawn painted the sky in oranges and pinks, I sat cross-legged on my sofa, notebook open on my lap, and mapped out all we had on the case. The SIA had been focusing on the murders; the human hunts were almost an afterthought. Yet, they had to be connected. We just needed to find out how. Chasing Nate all over the city to bring him in for questioning wouldn't bring us any closer to finding out what was going on. We needed something concrete, and intuition told me the human hunts and auctions were where our attention should be.

I woke up several hours later, stretched out on the sofa, my notebook on the floor, and my doorbell buzzing. Groaning, I made my way to the intercom by the front door and pressed the button.

"Yeah?"

"It's me." Carter's voice boomed out of the speaker.

"Come on up." I pressed the button to unlock the main door downstairs and give Carter entry to the building. I stood waiting in the doorway, leaning against the frame as the elevator made its way to my floor. Carter stepped out, looking fresh in his blue jeans, a white T-shirt, and thrown over the top, a checkered red-and-white button-down.

"You're looking good." The compliment tumbled out. I blamed my sleep-fogged brain.

"Thank you. You look like you just woke up."

"I did. Fell asleep on the sofa. Put the coffee on

while I freshen up, will ya?" I was already heading up the stairs to my bedroom. The front door clicked shut, and I could hear him puttering around in the kitchen. After taking care of my bladder, I quickly ran a brush through my hair, leaving it loose to fall over my shoulders. Splashing water over my face, I dried off and quickly changed into fresh jeans and a T-shirt before returning downstairs.

"So, to what do I owe the pleasure?" I slid onto a stool at the breakfast bar and pulled the steaming cup of coffee he'd just placed in front of me closer to my chest.

"Well. It's my birthday in a few days, and the pack is throwing a BBQ. I wanted to stop by and invite you in person."

"Your birthday again already?" I made a mental note to make sure to buy him a gift. "And sure, I'd love to come. Just tell me what time and what to bring."

"Next Tuesday, when we're in swing shift." Swing shift was the four days off between day and night shifts. "And you don't need to bring anything. The females of the pack go crazy with the food."

I laughed. I'd been to several social events with Carter's pack, and it was true; they catered for hundreds. I always came home with my arms full of leftovers.

"So, this couldn't wait until shift tonight?" I teased, sipping my coffee. He looked sheepish, gazing into his cup before meeting my eyes.

"I feel bad things have been a bit off with us lately. Tense. I wanted to clear the air."

"We're okay, Carter. We'll always be okay, you know that, right? Just because you get all pissy every now and then—"

"Hey!" He cut me off. "I swear to God, half the time, you do stuff just to antagonize me."

"That's possibly true." I winked and took another sip of my coffee, unable to hide my smile.

"Bitch," he grumbled, but he smiled back. Pulling something out of his back pocket, he placed it on the counter in front of me.

I sucked in a sharp breath. It couldn't be…it was! The latest release of my favorite video game, *Storm Girl*.

"Oh, you clever, clever boy!" I squealed, throwing one arm around his neck in a quick hug before snatching the game up in my hand and racing to the entertainment unit, coffee forgotten. I tossed him the second controller and plopped myself in my usual spot on the sofa, waiting impatiently as the game scrolled through the opening credits.

The cushion dipped as he sat next to me, and I planted a wet kiss on his cheek and said, "Thank you"—all without my eyes leaving the screen.

"You're welcome." He laughed, knowing this game was my weakness. I'd racked up too many hours to admit to over the years, and I loved that he knew me so well. This was the best gift he could ever give me. The game itself and playing it with me. He was a true friend.

We played for the rest of the afternoon until my alarm went off. Time to get ready for work. I rushed upstairs for a quick shower and changed into my uniform. Carter had his in the car, saying he'd change at work. While I was getting ready, he thumbed through the notebook with my thoughts on the case.

"So, I was thinking about the case, going over the stuff you have here..." He dropped the notebook back onto the coffee table. "We still need to bring Wilder in, but you and I know it won't give us the answers we're looking for. So, in the meantime, what do you think of checking out Wolf Hill? Try to find that cave where the humans were being held. What do you think?"

"Can't hurt. We can do a run-by of the club and Nate's home first. Maybe he's turned up. That should keep the Director off our backs, at least."

"Agreed."

We managed to avoid the director at the office, logged our plans, then did a drive-by to Crimson Mist and Nate's house in the Garden District. Naturally, they hadn't seen him and didn't know where he was. They were lying, of course. Then, we headed out to Wolf Hill. Wolf Hill was more than a hill; it was acres of land and mountain ranges where the wolves, well, anyone, for that matter, could run, hike, and camp. Humans and supernaturals used the land, but mostly the wolves used it.

We drove as far as we could, parking in the last car park up the mountainside. The air was crisp, and my breath came out in white puffs. I shivered, pulling my heavy winter coat around me and zipping it to my chin. I pulled a red-knitted beanie from my pocket and pulled it over my head, tucking my hair under as well. Carter's mom had knitted it for me last winter, and while it wasn't standard uniform, it came in handy at times like this.

Carter grabbed his backpack and tossed me mine. I rummaged inside for my night vision goggles.

"Follow me. Stay close behind, and don't trip over anything." I was happy to oblige. Up here in the dark, I was virtually blind without the goggles. I didn't possess wolf vision like he did. He'd once told me that his night vision wasn't that much different from daylight. He had the same definition and clarity; it just looked like a black-and-white movie.

Carter pulled out an evidence bag from his backpack. Inside was the T-shirt the wolf Miller wore the night we arrested him. He'd been up here, and chances were Carter would be able to catch his scent and track where he went. He held the T-shirt up to his nose and breathed deeply, closing his eyes. After a moment, he shoved the T-shirt back into the plastic bag, sealed it, and returned it to his backpack.

"This way."

"You picked up his scent already?" Amazing.

"Only slight. There's been a lot of activity up here, but I got a very faint trace. We need to move away from the car park and go deeper. Hopefully, I'll get a stronger lead."

"Lead the way." I pulled the goggles into place, and the world took on a green hue.

"Try and watch where you're walking. We don't need to advertise we're up here, although Lord knows they'll hear you tramping through the woods."

"Pft. I'm as light as a feather."

"Not to a wolf's sensitive ears, you aren't."

As I followed Carter into the woods, the trees blocked out what little light there was, and I was grateful for the magic of night-vision lenses. But even with them, I was glad I had Carter to follow. He moved through the night with ease. And speed. If I'd been alone, I'd be a lot slower.

"Stop," he whispered. I stopped immediately. Carter was motionless in front of me. He reached back, grabbed hold of my hand, and attached it to the belt loop of his pants.

"Don't let go. And keep quiet."

"Okay."

"Ssshh."

Right. Crouching slightly, he began moving forward. I followed, trying to be as quiet as possible, but I couldn't see much, even with the goggles. He kept stopping, and I kept bumping into him. Each time I did, I'd mutter, "Shit. Sorry." And he'd hush me.

I heard him breathe in deeply through his nose. He'd caught the scent. He moved forward again, fast, and my fingers slipped from his belt loop. *Shit.*

Hurrying after him, my arms outstretched in the dark, it dawned on me that I couldn't hear him anymore. My fingers brushed the bark of a tree to my left, then to the right. I thought I heard a twig snap up ahead, so I hurried my pace to catch up. It had been a long time since I'd used night-vision goggles, and now I remembered why. I hated them. Everything was green and unfamiliar, confusing my brain. I couldn't tell a person from a tree!

Suddenly my goggles were wrenched from my face. What the hell? I froze, holding my breath. Nothing. Not a sound. And without the goggles, I was blind. It was so damn dark out here. That's when I ran face-first into a tree and promptly ricocheted off and onto my ass. Forehead stinging from the contact with the rough bark, I scrambled back to my feet. I badly wanted to turn on the torch I had stashed in my backpack, but that would give us away—if I hadn't already—if the hunters were out here tonight.

Something brushed past my cheek, and I sucked in my breath, holding it to quell the startled squeal that almost escaped. *Whoosh.* Again, on the other side. I spun, arms out, but of course, I couldn't see a damn thing. Someone was here. Someone was playing with me.

I raised my hand, ready to release my power. I'd freeze any son of a bitch who tried to get near me. But what if I incapacitated Carter? And now that I was all turned around, I didn't know what direction he'd gone. My fingers uncurled, my hand dropping to my side.

Snap. Off to my left. I swung around, squinting into the darkness. Then, suddenly, I was propelled backward until my back hit the trunk of a tree. Nate. He was here. He had me pinned up against the tree, his body flush with mine. His hand wrapped around the back of my neck, his thumb stroking the sensitive skin under my jaw.

"What are you doing?" I whispered.

"Isn't it obvious?" His breath in my ear made me shiver. The guy didn't take no for an answer, and the thought crossed my mind that I was very vulnerable, out here in the dark, alone, with a vampire pinning me to a tree.

Perhaps he felt how rigid I'd become, or maybe good sense finally penetrated his thick skull because he eased back, putting some space between us.

"Please don't." My words were soft. I thought he'd known from the last time he kissed me that I wasn't into him, so his actions tonight surprised me.

He cursed, and then he was gone.

"Black?" Carter was returning.

"Here." Our voices were hushed. Within seconds he was by my side, clasping my hand in his.

"Stay close. Someone's out here."

I swallowed. I already knew someone was out there. Nate Wilder. Carter leaned in close, so close our noses were practically touching. I could barely make out his face in the darkness.

"I see Wilder found you."

"Oh." He knew. Of course, he knew, with his wolfy senses, he'd have known Nate was here before I did.

"Are you...bleeding?" Disbelief colored his voice. "Did that bastard bite you?"

"What? No!" I raised my spare hand to my forehead where I'd nailed myself with the tree. I had an egg-sized lump, and the skin felt damp and grazed.

"I ran into a tree. Scratched my forehead."

"Typical. And where are your night vision goggles? There's a wolf out here. Stay behind me. Hopefully, I can block your scent, but it's going to be harder with the smell of your blood in the air. This time don't let go."

After a few minutes of Carter dragging me through the woods, he stopped, turned to me, and pushed me over. What the hell? I landed with an oomph on my butt.

"You're slowing me down. Stay here. Literally right here, on the ground. Pull your hat down over that cut. And for the love of God, just once, do what I say."

"Okay," I whispered back. Considering I'd followed his orders all evening, I didn't see what he was so pissy about.

It was spooky in the woods with no light, and I shivered. Straining my ears, I couldn't hear a thing. Where was Carter? Where was the wolf he was tracking? And where was Nate? Was he tracking the wolf too? Or us? The darkness and silence were closing in, and I was about to scramble to my feet and go and investigate when Carter returned.

"Lost him. But he dropped this." The glow from his hand indicated a mobile phone. Thankful for even a little bit of light, I jumped up and peered at it.

"Pretty basic. A burner, probably."

"I'd say so. Let's head back and get this to the lab. I don't think we'll get much else out here tonight. Especially now they know we're looking."

I shivered, rubbing my palms across my frozen cheeks as we walked. It was cold out. Even in my coat and hat, I was freezing, my feet blocks of ice. I was visibly shaking by the time we reached the car.

"Geez, look at you." Carter wrapped his arms around me and pulled me close, rubbing his hands up and down my back.

"F...f...freezing."

"Let's get you warmed up. Hop in." He pulled open the passenger door and boosted me inside, reaching over to snap the seatbelt in place when my fumbling fingers couldn't manage the task. I heard him rummaging around in the back of the car before he jumped into the driver's seat and gunned the engine.

"Here." He handed me a thermos, and my laughter barked out. He really was a boy scout, thinking of everything. I carefully poured myself a cup of the steaming coffee he'd packed, sighing aloud when the hot fluid slid down my throat and warmed me from the inside out. We drove back to town with the heater cranked to the max.

TWELVE

I was braiding my hair, getting ready for Carter's BBQ, when my phone vibrated its way across the top of my dresser. Snatching it up, I glanced at the screen. *Private number*. Hitting connect, I squeezed the phone between my ear and shoulder while juggling tying off my braid.

'Ello?"

"Sorry if I crossed the line." Nate's voice was as clear as he was standing in the room with me.

"You need to hand yourself in." I ignored his apology.

"That's not going to happen."

"Then I don't accept your apology."

"I didn't do this."

"So you say. But running from us doesn't look good for you."

"I'm not going to sit and rot in some cell waiting for you to prove I'm innocent."

"No one said you were under arrest. We just want to question you."

"You already did that."

"Formally. On the record. With cameras and all that jazz."

"Why do I get the feeling that once I step foot inside the SIA, I won't be leaving again in a hurry?"

"I don't know. Why do you get that feeling?"

He blew a sigh into the phone. "I need to prove that I didn't do this. I'm not involved. I can't do that if you lock me away."

"Yeah, yeah, yeah. You sound like a broken record. Look, was there a point to this call? And speaking of, how did you get my number?"

"I have my ways." He chuckled. "I've been counting the days since I ran into you in the woods."

"Stalker." I wasn't sure what Nate wanted from me. He was interested, I got that from how he kept kissing me, yet surely he could feel the lack of chemistry?

"Did you find anything useful on that phone?"

"How do you know about the phone?"

"I was watching. And I know the SIA has staked out a certain area of the woods."

"Then why ask if you already know?"

"I wanted to hear it from you."

"And you know I can't discuss the case with you, Nate. So, the question remains. Why the call?"

The phone clicked in my ear. He'd hung up. Tossing the phone onto the bed, I shimmied into a pair of blue jeans, pulled on a long-sleeved red T-shirt with the word "Weird" emblazoned on the front, and shoved my feet into my knee-high boots. I thought about what Nate had said, that he'd been watching us stake out the woods over the last few days. It had been a waste of time. No one had turned up; we had nothing new to go on. The coordinates found on the phone could have been from an old hunt, for all we knew, although the director had insisted the stakeout continue. Thankfully Carter and I had tonight off. It was McConnell's and Richards's turn to freeze their asses off.

Sliding down the banister, I swept up my black, fur-trimmed parka and headed out the door. Carter's birthday bash was going to be a blast. Werewolf celebrations always were.

More than a dozen cars were parked haphazardly around Carter's house when I arrived.

He lived a few minutes out of town, the rear of his property backing onto Wolf Hill. Convenient for a wolf.

Out the back, a huge bonfire raged, the flames dancing at least six feet into the air. Standing around the fire, beers in hand, were the male members of Carter's pack. I knew from experience that all the women would be inside, having commandeered the kitchen and churning out enough food to feed an army. I knew which group I belonged to. Veering over to the cooler near the back step, I grabbed myself a beer and joined the boys.

"Hey, Raven. How ya doing?" I was greeted by hugs and slaps on the back that nearly face-planted me into the ground. I grinned at them.

"Aww, you guys." I'd known Carter's pack almost as long as I'd known him—and they were forever taking me under their wing. Their closeness and camaraderie used to make me yearn to join their pack too, to wish I were a wolf, but then I'd see the segregation of male and female, the submissive ways of the women, and quickly decided a pack was not the place for me.

"Happy birthday, Carter." I threw my arms around his neck and planted a wet kiss on his cheek.

His arms wrapped around me, and he held me tight, dropping a kiss on the top of my head.

"Thanks, trouble."

"Your present is in my car."

"What did ya get him? A blow-up doll?" one of the guys called out.

"Better. A subscription to that nudie magazine he likes so much." Hoots of laughter echoed around us, and Carter's cheeks blushed a becoming shade of red.

"You didn't!"

"No, you idiot. I got you that Scotch you like, the really old stuff. Since you're old now too."

"Raven! That Scotch is like a hundred and fifty bucks a bottle."

"Which is why it's in my car. To stop these idiots from drinking it. Remind me to give it to you before I leave."

He wrapped me in another hug, squeezing tight. Guess he really likes that Scotch.

"Oh. Sorry. I don't mean to interrupt...but..." a soft feminine voice came from behind me. Carter let go, and I moved to his side. The voice belonged to a petite blonde woman who was holding a tray of burgers.

"Thought you might be hungry," she continued,

stepping closer, her blue eyes trained on Carter. Then she glanced at me, and I swear to God, her gaze iced over. *Okaaaay.*

"Thanks, Storm, you're the best." Carter smiled at her and took a burger from the tray. "Storm, have you met Raven? Raven's my partner at the SIA. Raven, this is Storm, a member of our pack."

"Nice to meet you. I haven't seen you around before." I smiled at her, trying to put her at ease.

"I haven't seen you here before either." Her eyes had defrosted enough to shoot daggers at me. Okay, jealous little wolf, I'm not a threat. But by the way her eyes were devouring Carter, she definitely thought I was. And Carter, the big buffoon, had no idea.

"Here, let me take that from you, and you guys catch up." I took the tray from her hands before she could protest and moved around to the other side of the bonfire. The guys swarmed around me, snatching up the food, the tray empty in seconds. I stood and scrutinized Storm and Carter through the dancing flames; his dark head bent down to her blonde one, her hand resting on his arm as they talked. I didn't like the pang of jealousy that burned in my stomach. Nor did I like the fact that I couldn't keep my eyes off him.

Dressed in blue jeans and a thick brown jacket, he looked every inch the rugged mountain man, and again, he took my breath away. I watched as Carter's Alpha, Travis, headed over to him, shook his hand, and wrapped him in a bear hug.

"Good to see you, man. Happy birthday!"

"Good to see you too. Thanks for coming." Carter accepted the beer Travis held out, taking a long swig before leveling his gaze on me. I wish I could blame the sudden flush of heat in my cheeks on the bonfire, but I'd only be lying to myself. This guy affected me in ways I'd never experienced before. He was like a magnet, and I was inexplicably drawn to him. Unfortunately, the same was true for Storm, who crowded and fussed, offering food, hugs, and kisses. He accepted her attention with good grace, returning hugs, dropping kisses on her cheek or the top of her head, accepting food, and complimenting the women on their hard work. I viewed it all through the blaze of the fire. As he made his way around the fire to where the guys were standing, I'd inch my way around to the opposite side, keeping the flames between us.

"He's a handsome man, isn't he?" April Harper, the Alpha's wife, appeared by my side, watching the men through the fire.

"He sure is," I agreed.

"You do know that he can't be with you, though, right?"

"What do you mean?" I didn't like the way April was regarding me. Was that pity in her eyes?

"Sweetheart, you know the ways of the pack. Alex will settle down with his mate, a wolf. I think Storm is the perfect match for him."

"He's my best friend, not my boyfriend!" I forced a laugh and turned from the fire to find another beer, uncomfortable with the conversation. The women of his pack felt the need to warn me off Carter. Always had. In the past, I'd laughed it off, not letting it bother me. But tonight, it bothered me because April was right. Something had changed between Carter and me. Maybe April had known it all along, maybe not. Popping the top off another beer, I took a long swallow, wishing the beer was something more substantial. I needed something to take the edge off these damn emotions.

"You're avoiding me."

The beer went down the wrong way, and I coughed, choking. Carter's large hand thumped my back as my eyes streamed. *Great. Not embarrassing at all.*

"Better?" He leaned forward, peering into my

face, one hand pushing the hair that had escaped my braid out of my face. God, I couldn't think when he was this close to me. It was like I couldn't function—my thought processes stopped, my hormones raged, I felt totally out of control, and it terrified me.

"I'm fine." I cleared my throat and moved back a fraction. His fingers trailed through my hair before his arm dropped to his side.

"I get the feeling the womenfolk are giving you a hard time." His lip turned up in a wry smile. I shrugged, refusing to meet his eyes.

"You're nervous of me." He frowned, his face full of concern.

"You make me feel things I've never felt before," I admitted.

"Ah." He nodded solemnly. "And it scares you?" He didn't seem surprised by my admission.

"It does. And confuses me."

"How so?"

"Because up until recently, we've been friends. Just friends. And now everything is changing."

"You don't need to fear change."

Possibly. But it felt somehow different. Deeper. And given that I didn't know my past, my history, it rattled me. I liked the familiar. I liked knowing where I stood, my place in the world, where I felt safe. This growing...whatever it was between Carter and me had me off balance and unnerved.

"I won't hurt you," he promised.

"You think that's why I'm afraid? That you'll hurt me?"

"Isn't it?"

"There's something you need to know about me."

"Oh? I've known you most of my adult life, Raven. I doubt there is anything about you that I don't already know."

"I don't do relationships. Yes, I admit, I'm so wildly attracted to you, that I'd jump your bones in a heartbeat with no second thought. But then that would be it. It would be over. And so would our friendship. And you mean too much to me to allow that to happen." At my words, his heat flared. I felt it wrap around me, encompass me. *How did he do that?*

"Just so you know..." He leaned in close, his mouth next to my ear, his hot breath bathing my skin. "I don't do one-night stands."

I turned my head slightly so my cheek touched his. We stood there, our heads close together, skin brushing skin, carnal thoughts dancing through my mind. It was torture and bliss.

"When you jump my bones and don't worry baby, it's going to happen, and soon, one night isn't going to be enough for you." His words were a promise, and I trembled. His hand came up to cup my cheek and tilt my head further, our mouths meeting. He tasted like I remembered. Hot and sweet. This time his kiss was slow and gentle, not the hurried, urgent mating of our mouths like last time. This was the second time he kissed me, and each time was different yet still blistering hot.

We broke apart to cheers and jeers from the pack. Christ, I'd forgotten we had an audience. Carter's hand was still on my neck as I turned my head and looked toward the bonfire. Storm was there, watching. I waited for her reaction, figured she'd be angry I was making out with Carter. I was right. She whirled from the fire, storming inside with April hot on her heels, throwing us a glare as she swept past.

"It will be okay," Carter muttered, but the frown pulling his brows together told me he didn't believe it any more than I did.

THIRTEEN

Turned out the mobile phone we'd found was a burner, just like we'd suspected. No stored contacts and only one text message, a bunch of numbers that turned out to be longitude and latitude coordinates to Wolf Hill.

The four days we'd been on swing shift, the day shift Enforcers had scoured Wolf Hill, turning up nothing. I sat at my desk, tapping my fingers. I needed to bring Nate Wilder in. This was somehow linked to him. I could have sworn the human hunts and the murders were connected, but now I was starting to doubt myself. Was it merely a coincidence, and I'd been wasting precious time? Time that was running out for the next potential victim?

"Hey." Carter dropped down into his chair, his brown eyes meeting mine.

"Hey." We hadn't spoken since the kiss at his party. Oh, there had been plenty of missed calls and voicemails. All of which I'd deleted without listening to. Immature perhaps, but I'm big on avoidance when it comes to emotional stuff, and the glimpse I'd just caught of Carter's face showed he was full to the brim with emotion. *Oh boy*.

Raising my coffee to my lips, I took a hefty sip. A new Pixie was working at the Witches Brew, and she'd introduced a range of coffees filled with elemental spices. Today my coffee was laced with focus. Yesterday, I had clarity.

"What happened to your hand?" he asked. I glanced at the bandage wrapped around the palm of my left hand.

I shrugged. "Cut myself on some glass. Needed stitches."

"Is that why you didn't answer my calls? Because you were at medical?"

Partly. Carter and I had always been truthful with each other if not a little blunt, and I couldn't see a reason to change now.

"After your party, I went home and drank a bottle of vodka—"

"On your own?" he cut in.

"On my own. Naturally, that made me not only hungry but also extremely inebriated. While making myself a snack, my glass slipped. It broke in my hand."

"Were you trying to make cheese toasties one-handed again? When you're drinking alone, you know that no one is going to steal or spike your drink, right? You can actually put it down."

"And this is why I didn't bother calling you. The lectures."

"Continue." He waved his hand in a please proceed gesture.

"I got a cab to medical, where they stitched me up. Came home, went to bed, and woke up with the most god-awful hangover. I spent all day on the sofa regretting the vodka, then thought I'd check out Crimson Mist to see if Wilder had turned up."

"You went to Crimson Mist? Alone? Without backup?"

I raised my eyebrows, nailing him with a cold, hard stare. *See? Lectures.*

"I went as a patron. To have fun." And to case the joint. Not only for Nate but for anything, any clue that would give me a lead in finding the murderer.

"And did you? Have fun?"

"I did." Not entirely true. I'd been curious about the pheromones they pumped into the air, curious to see if there was a hot, sexy man who could take the edge off the tension that, thanks to Carter, had not left me since our encounter in the club. And although I'd stayed until dawn, no such thing occurred. Plenty of hot, sexy-looking guys, but none of them caught my interest.

"So, after spending all night at the club, I had yet another hangover to sleep off. Yesterday I spent most of the day at the Witches Brew."

"Where was your phone in all of this?" The suspicious frown he leveled at me made me grin. He knew me well.

"I found my phone in the fridge," I admitted.

"So you weren't avoiding my calls then?"

"To be honest, I was. But when I lost my phone, well, let's say I didn't search very hard," I snarled, my patience as frayed as the worn edges of our friendship.

"Why dodge me?" he shot back, his voice slicing through the tension. "We need to hash out that kiss; the one you're pretending didn't set your world on fire."

His words were a challenge, thrown down between us like a gauntlet. "Fine, you want the raw truth?" I said, my voice scaling up with my panic. "That kiss—it scared the hell out of me. Because it wasn't just a kiss, not with you."

He stood, a force of nature that filled the room. "I'm all in," he declared, his voice a blend of desire and certainty.

I paced like a caged animal, the space between us electric. "And I'm all over the place," I admitted, the admission scraping my throat raw. "I'm terrified, Carter. Terrified that if we jump into this, into 'us,' I'll be the disaster that burns it all down."

I could almost see the picture he painted in his head—us, together, a team. But my imagination was darker, splattered with the ink of my past. I'd seen how these things play out, the blaze of passion that fizzles into resentment. One misstep and we'd be nothing but ash.

"I want you," he said, each word a pulse of the undeniable chemistry between us.

"And I want to run," I whispered, the truth lancing through me. "Because when this goes up in flames, when you look at me with hate where love once was, it'll be the end of me. You're my rock, Carter. Without you, I'd be lost."

It was the rawest of truths; the heart of my fear lay bare between us.

He dragged a hand down his face, the rough sound of stubble a faint whisper in the tense air of the office. "Hate isn't something I'm capable of when it comes to you," he said with a weary resolution. "The pack has been breathing down my neck, demanding my attention every moment since that night. If it weren't for their interference, I'd have been camping at your door until you let me in. And you can't blame it all on me—you hot-footed it out of there pretty fast."

The truth of his words was like a slap; the memory of fleeing from his unexpected public display of affection stung. " Because what you did—kissing me in front of your pack—was stupid. You put me in a position. You manipulated me. And I didn't, don't, appreciate it."

"I'm sorry," he offered, the words seeming to carry the weight of unspoken promises.

I needed space, a moment to disentangle my thoughts from the tight knot they had become. I snatched my jacket off the back of my chair, the fabric rustling loudly in the charged silence. Carter reached for his own, and I felt my frustration boil over. "I need to breathe," I said, a hard edge to my voice. "Alone." My gaze was fiery, a silent challenge, a demand for solitude.

"No can do. We need to get up to Wolf Hill and continue the search. There's a cave up there somewhere. We need to find it. We've got nothing else to go on, might as well chase down that lead."

He had a point, and that irritated me even more. Stalking to the elevator, I punched the button, leaving him to sign us out and grab the keys to the SUV. Our fellow Enforcers hadn't been able to locate the cave. What made Carter think we'd have any luck? What did he know that the others didn't?

I headed to the driver's side, frowning at Carter. "Keys?"

"No way, woman. I've seen you drive when you're angry. You're not getting behind the wheel."

"Are you serious?"

"Sit back and enjoy the ride, Spitfire."

"Fine." Sliding into the passenger seat, I snapped my seatbelt into place, ignoring him. He started the car and smoothly maneuvered out into the street. The close proximity in the car made me hyper-aware of him; his energy, his aura scraped over my skin like sandpaper.

"For what it's worth—" he began.

"Don't!" I cut him off. "I don't want to talk. You're going to make it worse."

"I missed you." His words were gruff. Heartfelt. I

turned my face away, staring blindly out the window, seeing nothing.

"We usually hang out a time or two between shifts. To not see you for four days was torture."

"Pft."

He blew out a sigh. "I stuffed up, okay? I shouldn't have kissed you—" I swiveled to look at him. If he was going to say he regretted kissing me, I would punch him in the face. My fingers clenched in readiness. "—in front of the pack. That was just stupid." He shook his head, thumping the steering wheel in apparent frustration. My fingers relaxed.

"Why did you?" My voice came out softer than I expected.

"I couldn't *not* kiss you. Your scent was all around me. All I could think about was you, the taste of you, your lips on mine, the rush of my blood when your tongue strokes mine, the little noises of pleasure that you make. That's all I could think of. I wasn't trying to manipulate you or trick you. I just had to kiss you."

My cheeks heated. This was dangerous. My anger had dissolved at his words, replaced by a tingling in my lady parts—what he described was what I wanted too. Badly. But the aftermath was too high a price to pay. I tamped down the lust, shoved it into a little box deep inside, and turned the key, determined to keep it buried and locked away forever.

The rest of the drive was in silence. I sensed each time he glanced my way, the warmth of his gaze almost a physical caress. I didn't know what he expected me to say. That it was okay? That his kisses unraveled me?

"Why don't you just say it?"

"What?" I gasped, swiveling my head so fast I almost gave myself whiplash. *Had he read my mind?*

"Whatever is playing through that pretty little head of yours, just say it." His fingers tightened on the steering wheel for the briefest of moments before relaxing.

"I can't."

"Why not?"

I shrugged. Because it was akin to opening Pandora's Box? Or a can of worms? Because I didn't want things to change, yet they were changing anyway, and I was being dragged, kicking and screaming, onto a new path. A path I was convinced would be our undoing!

"Your friendship means more to me than anything else in the entire world," I began, then stopped, unsure how to proceed.

"You think you'll lose it." His head nodded. "That we won't be able to be friends anymore."

"Because you want too much of me, Carter. You want it all, and you, of all people, should know that I don't have it to give. You'll be disappointed. And then it'll be too late; we won't be able to go back from lovers to friends. It never works that way."

"You have everything I need," he muttered, pulling into the parking lot and killing the engine. Neither of us moved.

"Let's just be real for a second, okay? What if, and this is a massive what if, what if we did hook up? Had a relationship. Fell in love. What then? Your pack would not accept me. Not as your mate. Never. I'm not a wolf. I bet they were busting your balls over that kiss. Am I, or am I not, correct?"

His hesitation, the subtle hint of color on his cheeks, told me I was right.

"Yeah. That's what I thought." Sliding out of the car, I restrained myself from slamming the door closed. *Fuck, it was cold up here.* Shivering, I hurried to the rear of the SUV and grabbed my coat from where I'd thrown it earlier. Pulling on gloves and hat, I avoided eye contact with Carter and stood out of the way while he got our supplies organized. I could see the cogs turning behind his eyes and knew he wasn't done with our conversation. I waited. Eventually, it came.

"You know I love you, right?"

"Like a sister," I added.

"No. Nothing like a sister. I'd be arrested if I had thoughts about my sister like I'm having about you." He chuckled.

"Fine. Not like a sister. You love me, but you're not in love with me." Please don't let him go there, I prayed. My hopes plummeted when he shook his head.

"Nope. I'm in love with you."

"Why are you telling me this?" I cried. "It's not going to change anything!"

"Because, for me, it did change everything! And you need to know because no matter how often you push me away, shut me down, say no, I am not giving up. I may not have all the answers yet, but I do know I love you, and you...mean the world to me. I'll do anything to keep you in my life."

I backed up a step when he moved closer. Undeterred, he grabbed my wrist.

"I get it. You're terrified. I'm betting you've never loved anyone or anything before. But you love me, Raven. You just don't know it yet." I tugged at my wrist, and he let me go. "I'm offering a truce: no more kissing, but I'm not giving up. You need time and space. You got it. I'll be waiting. Deal?"

Jesus Christ, how did he know me so well? It was almost creepy how he seemed to know me better than I knew myself. He voiced his feelings and emotions and wasn't scared to put himself out there and make himself vulnerable. It was the most endearing thing he could have ever done.

"Truce," I agreed, my voice rough.

I stuck out my hand to shake. He grabbed it and jerked me off balance into his arms. His mouth came down on mine, and I melted. With no hesitation, I opened my mouth, allowing him entry. His tongue danced with mine, the taste of him intoxicating. Raising my hands, I cradled his face, slowly ending the mind-drugging kiss. We stood, his forehead resting against mine, catching our breath.

"I thought we just declared a truce?" I breathed, my breath mingling with his.

"I think I may have lied," he admitted with a sheepish grin. "I meant it at the time." As if that was any consolation. Truth be told, I didn't want him to not kiss me. It confused the shit out of me.

Resting his hands on my shoulders, he straightened, then stepped back, releasing me. He sucked in a deep breath and blew it out, then smiled.

"Let's go find that cave."

"What makes you think we can find it? The guys have had days to search, and they still haven't turned up anything."

"I know Wolf Hill pretty well, and the coordinates on that phone do not lead to an area where a cave is likely. Just woods. So I got to thinking they still needed coordinates to direct buyers to the auction, but they have to be careful just in case the coordinates got into the wrong hands. My theory is we add a little extra to the coordinates. Say five degrees. Because five degrees west, there are hills and quite possibly caves."

"Aren't you the smart wolf?" I smiled.

FOURTEEN

Carter was right. We found the cave, further down the mountain than we'd anticipated, closer to civilization. Inside, three empty cages. The cages were large enough to house a big dog—barely big enough to hold a human. It made my blood boil to think of the terrified people who'd been forced into the cages, scared, unable to move, fearing for their lives. And they'd be right to be afraid.

We'd dragged the cages back to the SUV and dropped them off at the lab. One thing I'd noticed in each of the cages was a considerable amount of red dust in the bottom, which I guessed was transference from the captives' clothing.

"We found the cave. Clearly, they're not where

the auctions are held." I leaned back in my chair, frowning at my monitor. I'd logged the details of our find on Wolf's Hill, and while we were making progress, it wasn't fast enough. I was worried something terrible was about to happen. Another abduction, maybe? And I still wasn't one hundred percent sure they were linked. Was I grasping at straws, wanting everything tied up in a neat little bow?

"Definitely not. That place could barely fit the three cages, let alone a group of assholes bidding on humans. The cave has to be the holding place for the wolves after they've purchased their humans."

"Which still leaves us with the question of where the auctions are being held. And are they related at all to the murders of our four half-transformed victims?"

"The red dust could help. My guess is red brick dust. The lab will confirm." Carter's chair squeaked as he leaned back, linking his hands behind his head. He gazed up at the ceiling, deep in thought.

I tried to drag my eyes away; I really did, but it was hopeless. He was a magnet—every time I was within his orbit, I was drawn to him. The moment replayed in my head—a snapshot from that mountain conversation when he threw down the love card. It hit me like a sucker punch, that four-letter word I'd dodged all my life. Love? It was more alien to me than the supernatural creatures I dealt with daily. No one had ever slung those words at me before, and they landed heavy, like a gut punch, leaving me winded, clueless. It was a damn grenade he'd lobbed into my routine of solitude, and it left me scrambling—do I dive for cover, or do I throw it back? Did I love Carter? I wasn't sure. I sure liked him a lot. I enjoyed spending time with him. I missed him when he wasn't around. My body came alive whenever he touched me. And his kisses blew my mind. Was that love?

My comms unit buzzing startled me out of my thoughts, and I quickly answered. It was the lab.

"The red dust in the cages is brick dust, but it's old. From handmade bricks that were common about a hundred years ago," the tech told me, not bothering with niceties.

"Okay."

"But, on a hunch, I tested our four victims' clothing and found traces of the same dust."

"So, what you're saying is that wherever those bricks are, all four of our victims have been there as well? Most likely held or killed there."

"Affirmative. I'm running the results through the

database to see if we can narrow down what buildings were built in Redmeadows with those bricks. I'll send it through when it's done."

"Thank you." I glanced up at Carter, who was looking at me with one brow arched. "You heard? They found the same dust that was in the cages on our victims' clothing. The auctions and our murders are related."

"What are you thinking? That the victims were abducted, auctioned off, and whoever bought them killed them? In a weird, bizarre way?"

"Sounds plausible."

"We need to find out more about these auctions. Why don't we have more missing person reports? There were three cages in that cave, indicating the wolves could purchase a maximum of three humans for their hunting games. That tells me more people would have to be auctioned off to cater to the vampires and anyone else. Miller said even humans were buying humans."

"Let's go talk to Miller again."

***

"I TOLD YOU ALL I KNOW." Miller strode back and forth, agitated. He ran his fingers around the glowing collar secured around his neck. I'd allowed him to shift at the last full moon, but he'd been restrained in a silver-barred cell, couldn't run, hunt, or eat fresh meat. Once the change was over, his collar was put back on. His wolf was suffering because of it.

"You've been to at least one of these auctions?" Carter asked, voice like steel.

"Not to buy. Just to help transport," Miller protested as if that made a difference.

"How many humans were up for auction?"

"I don't know, man, I couldn't really see. I was out back with the transport!" He ran his fingers through his tangled hair, wincing when they snagged.

"You would have taken a look, though," I interjected. "A sneaky peek at what was on offer. Your curiosity would have gotten the better of you. How many did you see?" He eyeballed me, angry that I had him pegged. Of course he watched the auctions; morbid curiosity demanded he do so.

"Do I have to use my powers on you?" I held up a hand, ready to levitate him and bang his head against the ceiling if I had to.

"No! No!" Lowering his head, he muttered under his breath, "Yeah, I might have seen more than I should have a time or two. But I didn't, you know, count them."

"Guess. More than five? More than ten?"

"I dunno, around ten, I guess." He slid onto his chair, defeated.

"And how often are the auctions held?"

"Look, I don't know, okay? I was just the grunt. Took what was paid for, transported it to the cave, and kept watch." I ground my teeth at the way he dismissed human life so casually. They weren't *its*; they were people.

"How often did you do that? Just the once? A couple of times? A dozen times?" Carter persisted.

"Probably every couple of months." Miller's head was low, voice sullen.

Carter and I looked at each other. Someone was snatching people off the streets, holding them until they'd accumulated enough to hold an auction. Ten people every two months, give or take. That was a lot of people unaccounted for.

"The homeless?" I suggested, ignoring Miller, who now appeared to be quietly sobbing.

"Could be. Someone who wouldn't be missed," Carter agreed, pushing to his feet.

I followed him to the door. "But our four victims —they don't fit that profile. They were reported missing or would have been if they hadn't turned up dead first."

"What do we know for sure?" Carter prompted. I stopped outside Miller's cell, waiting while Carter locked up behind us.

"Our victims were part of the auction," I replied.

"Were they?" Carter argued. "We know they were held at the same place the auction victims were."

"You're right. It doesn't mean they were put up for auction, but what it is telling us is that it was most likely the same people who were snatching people for the auctions that took them. So... a private buyer?"

Carter nodded. "That seems more likely. Their bodies looked like they'd undergone some fucked up medical experimentation. Someone who has the capability to do that most likely has the dollars to have their subjects acquired for them. Our victims may even have been targeted on purpose. Maybe they needed them fit and healthy. A homeless person or drug addict wouldn't be suitable."

"But we don't have anything more to go on," I muttered, following Carter back to the elevator. "The phone we found gave us the coordinates but nothing else. Miller gave us the name Brooks as the guy who texts them with the auctions' info, but we've got no lead on him. The sketch Miller gave us hasn't turned up any hits."

"We've got the bricks. The lab is running them through the database right now. With any luck, we'll have a list of buildings that still exist that were built with them."

"And Crimson Mist. All four of our victims visited the nightclub days before they were killed. Nate Wilder isn't responsible, but it looks like someone is trying to frame him."

"Right. So we go back and interview all the staff. Every last one. And then we go visit recently fired staff. Anyone with a grudge. Wilder's a damn fool for running." Carter cursed. "This would be so much easier if we could talk to him. He probably has a running list of enemies. It'd save us valuable time."

"I know," I said. I hadn't told Carter about Nate kissing me. I had the feeling my laid-back, easygoing wolf partner would not be pleased to learn of Nate's advances.

"How are we going to do this? We're on the day shift. Most of the people we want to talk to will be at the club after our shift ends."

"Cleaners and admin staff are most likely around

during the day. We'll start with them. Augustine and Darabi can swing by tonight and talk to everyone else. The manager, the guy with the multicolored mane of hair, what's his name? He seemed cooperative."

"Xavier Elizondo," I replied. And while he did seem agreeable when we searched the club, who's to say he wasn't the one who planted the phone in Nate's desk? He certainly had the opportunity. There was no attempt to hide the phone. It was just thrown in the drawer, which made me think that whoever had put it there was in a hurry, that they weren't supposed to be there, and feared discovery. Maybe it was a member of staff, perhaps a patron. And if it was a patron, we were screwed. Unless! A thought hit me.

"Nate's IT lab." I grasped Carter's arm, voice urgent.

"What about it?"

"He has facial recognition software and all the footage from the club, all saved on his servers. What if we asked him to cross-reference the footage from the night each of our victims was there and see if we can create a list of people who were there on all four nights."

"Might be a big list. His club is popular." But the

look on his face told me he didn't hate the idea. "Trouble is, Nate is on the run."

"We don't need him. His IT guy, Ethan, can do it. I'm going to call him. Can't hurt to ask."

The lift opened on our floor, and I rushed to my desk, eager to call Ethan.

"Don't forget he's a vamp; he'll most likely be asleep." Carter vetoed his desk for the coffee machine.

"I'll leave a message. He'll help us if he wants to get his boss off the hook."

FIFTEEN

The thrill of finally having something to go on, a thread I could tug and watch unravel as the pieces fell into place, went a long way to keep my mind off of Carter. Mostly. We'd gone back to the Crimson Mist and started the interviews with the staff who were around during the day. But despite keeping busy, my mind kept drifting to Carter and his declaration on Wolf Hill. Crazy wolf thinking he was in love with me. But something took root the minute those words left his mouth because now, when I should be listening to what the woman in front of me was saying, my mind was playing images of what it was like to kiss Carter, the taste of him in my mouth...the promises of what was to come.

It suddenly registered that the woman had gone quiet and was standing there looking at me. She was one of the club's cleaners, decked out in a polo shirt uniform, cleaning trolley by her side.

"Sorry, I didn't catch that last bit," I admitted, biting my cheek. Keep your mind on the job, Raven!

"I said, no, I haven't seen anything unusual or out of the ordinary. I clean the bathrooms. No surprises there besides the usual."

"No outer doors left ajar; no windows left open?" I prompted.

"Nope. Nothing like that. Look, can I go now? I've got six bathrooms to clean before the club opens tonight. They ain't gonna clean themselves."

"Yeah, sure. Here, take my card. If you do see anything, anything at all, please call." I handed her my card, and she hurried off. She was my last interview of the day, and so far, we'd come up with nothing. I hoped Carter had more luck than me. My comms unit vibrated on my wrist, and I glanced at the screen: the lab was calling.

"Black," I answered.

"I've found something really interesting!" The lab technician's voice crackled with energy, a stark contrast to the usual monotone. It was clear he'd hit on something big, his words rushing out with the kind of raw enthusiasm usually kept under lab coats and behind stoic, professional facades.

"Hit me."

"The victims all have the same rare gene." He waited with bated breath as if I understood what that meant.

"So?" I had no clue.

He sighed with what I assumed was exasperation. "All four victims have had some medical experimentation done on them. From their physical appearance and the blood work results, it looks like someone is trying to blend species. From what I discovered today, their subject has to have a certain gene for that to be successful. A certain rare gene."

Now I understood. "That's how they are targeting their victims. But how would they know who has this gene and who doesn't?" I asked myself more than the tech, but he answered anyway.

"Dunno, that's your job, but I would say they most likely have access to medical records. Possibly work at a hospital or doctor's office."

"Or they hacked the hospital databases."

"Or that," he agreed. "Anyway, thought you should know. It could also help you find any more potential victims and, you know, warn them."

"Send your report. I'll subpoena hospital records when I return to HQ to see if we can find out who else has this gene."

Disconnecting the call, I looked up to see Carter approaching. My eyes drank in the way he walked, his long-legged stride. The second he realized I was watching, his step faltered for a nano-second before he continued toward me. Dragging my eyes from his body, I met his gaze. Dark. Swirling. Capturing me and pulling me in. Heat pooled in my stomach, my skin prickled, and all I could think about was getting him naked.

"Raven." He stopped in front of me, his voice a growl, and I shivered, wondering what it would be like to have his lips against my skin when he growled my name like that. "If you don't want me to kiss you senseless right here and now, you have to stop."

His words penetrated the sensual fog, and I dropped my eyes, looking intently at the stitching on his shirt inches from my face, trying not to be distracted by his chest and wanting to run my hands over it, feel the firm muscle I knew was hidden beneath the fabric.

"Fuck me." He cursed, and I snapped my head back up. His mouth came down on mine, hot, demanding, impatient. I wanted it, needed it, craved it. And so much more. I came alive in his arms—my blood pumped furiously, my skin super sensitive as if I'd been poked with a live wire, and my legs? My legs wanted to wrap around his waist and never let go. Tearing his lips from mine, he stepped back, hands on my shoulders to hold me away when I tried to move closer.

"What?" I was confused, my voice thick with lust. "I give in," I murmured now. "I want you so goddamn badly. The ache is painful."

"Same." He grunted, dragging in a harsh breath, struggling to regain his composure. "What I said earlier? Forget it. If sex is all you can offer me, I'll take it. I'll take anything as long as I can have you."

"You're sure?" His turnaround surprised me. Earlier, he'd been declaring his love and picturing a happily ever after, but now he'd done a one-eighty and was okay with my terms. A physical, non-emotional roll in the hay.

"I'm sure." Before he changed his mind, I grabbed his hand and, moving at lightning speed, led him outside to the car park behind Crimson Mist. Our SUV and two other cars were the only vehicles. We wouldn't be disturbed. I hoped.

"You want to do it here?" He sounded surprised,

and I glanced at him over my shoulder as I dug in my pocket for the keys and hit the remote to unlock the car.

"I cannot wait, Carter. I need to have you. I swear to God I'll die if I don't." As soon as the words left my mouth, I was spun and pinned to the side of the SUV. My wrists caught up on either side of my head, his large hands holding me there. He was plastered against me, his pelvis hard against mine, his mouth crushing my lips. I loved it. Every. Single. Second.

I was on fire, pretty sure I was in danger of self-combusting, but hell, what a way to go. His hands were everywhere, as were mine, tearing at clothing, desperate to touch.

Lifting one leg, I wrapped it around his hips, gasping into his mouth when he rocked against me. His hands left my wrists to cup my breasts through my shirt, and I arched into him at the contact, wrapping my arms around his neck, deepening our kiss, stroking him with my tongue while rubbing myself against the hardness in his pants. I felt him tug at my shirt, pulling it free from my pants; then his hands slid underneath, pushing my bra up until he was cupping me, flesh against flesh. I couldn't describe the sound I made, a combination of a sigh, a scream, and a demand for more.

Reaching between us, I got to work on his belt and zipper, wanting to feel him, to touch what I'd only ever dared to fantasize about. Freeing him from his boxer shorts, I delighted in the silky hardness of him in my palm, loving the shudder that wracked his frame when I curled my fingers around him and stroked.

"Raven." That low, resonant call of my name set a wildfire of sensation ablaze beneath my skin. My head tilted back instinctively, finding the cold, hard metal of the SUV, but the stark chill was a distant notion against the fever of his touch. "Here? Now?" His words, a hushed urgency against my throat, sent shivers down my spine.

"Absolutely. Don't you dare stop," I gasped, the plea mingled with a demand. His heat enveloped me, a consuming blaze I had no desire to escape. My hands fumbled a clumsy dance with my clothing, urgency overriding grace.

"Let me," he insisted, his movements deft, peeling away the barriers with an ease that spoke of a hunger as desperate as my own. One boot fell away, then trousers and panties pooled around my remaining ankle—a tangle of fabric that mattered less than the press of his body against mine.

I anchored him closer with a leg wrapped tightly around his waist, a moan spilling from my lips as his touch ignited every nerve. My hands found him, seeking to stoke his fire just as he fueled mine.

"You're so hot," he murmured, his mouth a breath from mine, the heat of his words fanning the flames. He was all sensation now, every touch a spark, every movement stoking the burn.

"Look at me," he commanded, a brief withdrawal that was both torment and tantalizing promise. Our gazes locked, a silent communion before he surged forward, and the world narrowed to the sheer intensity of him—of us. His eyes reflected a storm of desire, pupils dilated in the shadowed light, every thrust deepening the bond, the connection that threatened to overwhelm me.

The world around us ceased to exist as it became our anchor, our private cocoon where the rhythm he set consumed all thought. His lips sought to capture the sounds of my pleasure, but they spilled forth unbidden, a symphony of raw need. The line between us blurred, the heat of him melding seamlessly with the cool fire of my own awakening. In this maelstrom of sensation, I realized this was more than passion. It was a revelation, a seismic shift in my very being, powerful and unequivocal. I was lost in the depths of it, and at that moment, I couldn't have found my way out even if I'd wanted to.

Everything disappeared as I climbed higher and higher—my blood burned in my veins, my heart thundered in my chest, my skin slick with sweat, and still, I climbed, impossibly high until finally, I reached the summit. My orgasm tore through me. I wrenched my mouth from his and threw back my head, hitting the SUV hard as a hoarse yell left my mouth. He followed me over the edge until we were free-falling, stars dancing behind my closed lids as we danced and spun through the universe.

I didn't care that we were in the parking lot of a club in the middle of the afternoon where anyone could discover us. The plan had been a simple, fiery tangle in the backseat of the SUV, but the second his hands pinned me to its cool metal door, my intentions scattered like ash in a stiff breeze. We could've been stark naked and shameless under the broad daylight, for all it mattered to me at that moment. This wasn't a mere collision of bodies seeking solace from the storm. No, this was an entirely new storm—feral and all-consuming.

Every coherent thought vaporized, leaving behind a singular, pulsing truth: this intensity, this electric desire—was this the alchemy of being wanted, truly and deeply? If so, I was starved for it, craving the endless depths of this newfound fervor.

His voice broke through the satiated fog, a gentle prod back to reality. "We need to get moving." How long had we been melded against the SUV, my very bones turned to warm wax in his embrace?

"Ugh," was all that escaped me, a sound thick with the aftershocks of what had just transpired. Never before had I been so lost in the moment, so surrendered to the rush of desire. The sobering thought of our primal union being more than pleasure—a binding—sent a shiver through me.

My legs, though shaky, held my weight as I pulled back from his heat, feeling a pang of loss when his touch vanished. Then, a jolt of alarm cut through the haze. "We didn't use protection!"

"It's fine. I'm clean." His words came swiftly, laced with an assurance unique to our kind.

But my mind raced past the concern of disease to a more profound possibility. "And if I get pregnant?" The question hung between us, stark and heavy.

He blinked, taken aback. "Should that worry us? I can only reproduce with another wolf."

I fixed him with a look, the ground beneath us suddenly unsteady. "Because we don't know the first damn thing about what I am or what rules my body plays by," I said, a cold realization washing over me.

Silence stretched as he processed the magnitude of our oversight. "Right. I didn't consider that."

The frustration in my voice was sharper than I intended. "Well, it's a bit late now, isn't it?" I retrieved the keys, their clink sounding like a timer's bell, marking the end of our reckless reprieve. Climbing into the SUV, I couldn't escape the gravity of our actions. What had begun as an impulse now felt like an irreversible step into the unknown.

SIXTEEN

"What do you mean I have to have the tests re-done?" I stood before the director's desk, my body vibrating with anger. We'd made it back to HQ in record time. I'd successfully managed to avoid any conversation with Carter, even though he was itching to talk about what had just transpired between us. I, however, was not. Oh no. It was a mistake. A big, fat, colossal, totally hot, totally blew-my-mind mistake.

I'd been at my desk for all of two seconds when the summons from the director arrived. I was needed. Urgently.

"There was a malfunction with the cooling units," she explained calmly, steepling her fingers in front of her chin and looking at me with cold green eyes.

"So you've lost the samples you've already taken? That's what you're saying?" I couldn't believe it. The blood, the swabs, the spinal tap—all gone?

"Correct. We've lost the samples. I'm sorry, I know it's not the best outcome, but..." She shrugged, and again I sensed her apology was not sincere, not heartfelt in the slightest.

"Remind me again why I need these tests." Folding my arms across my chest, I eyeballed her. I still didn't buy that the Council was demanding I be classified. With everything else that was going on, this stank, right up there with dog shit and fish guts.

"We've been over this, Black. Report to medical. Immediately." Her voice was ice-cold, ruthless. I glared back at her for a moment before swiveling on my heel and stalking out with a grim sense of satisfaction when her door slammed shut behind me.

Back at my desk, I noisily flung my firearm and badge into my top drawer, securing them with a swipe of my pass.

"What's going on?" Carter asked. We had another three hours before our shift ended.

"Gotta go back to medical." I was seething,

furious over the need to have the painful procedures repeated. On top of my regret for giving in to my base instincts and shagging my best friend was the niggling feeling that something was up. Something other than the massive complication I'd just created in my life. A gut instinct that I couldn't ignore.

"What? Why?" Carter stopped what he was doing, his brows drawn together. He looked cute and adorable, and my anger crept up a notch.

"Apparently, there was a malfunction with the cooling units, and my previous samples were destroyed." I clenched my teeth so hard my jaw ached. I didn't want to do this. The blood I didn't mind so much, but the spinal tap? That hurt like a bitch and gave me a wicked headache. "I'll see you tomorrow. Can you follow up with Ethan about the footage from the club before you clock out?" I'd left a message for Ethan asking for his help, and I was working on the assumption that he'd help us if only to clear Nate's name. And I was trying to deflect Carter's attention away from me and back onto our case.

"Raven, hold up." Carter's voice was a hand on my shoulder, halting my escape towards the elevator. I could feel the heat of his gaze on me, searing through the distance.

I stopped but didn't turn to face him. "Not now, Carter," I said, my voice a low growl of tangled emotions. The chaos within me was a wildfire, untamed and all-consuming, fueled by our reckless coupling and the looming dread of medical tests.

There was a pause, a breath where I felt his hesitation. "Okay, good luck," he finally murmured, and I sensed rather than saw him retreat. The cool metal doors of the elevator closed, granting me the solitude I craved to nurse the raw edges of my frayed nerves.

Pushing my now very complicated relationship with Carter to the back of my mind, I focused on the Council's sudden urgency in determining my species. As I rode the elevator up to the car park, I knew there were two choices: submit to the testing and do what I was told, or visit the Council and demand to know what was happening. By the time I reached my car, my decision was made. Peeling out of the parking lot, I headed away from the medical lab and toward the city center. The Paranormal Council was located beneath the humans' City Council Chambers. It consisted of twelve Council members, each representing a different species, who governed over the paranormals. Pretty much like every paranormal service in the city, they operated in twelve-hour shifts to accommodate nocturnal and daywalker's needs as required.

"Do you have an appointment?" the fairy receptionist asked, one pencil-thin brow arched as she eyed me up and down.

"No. But I need to talk to the Council, and I'm not leaving here until I do." My anger bubbled just beneath the surface, and if I needed to unleash some whoop-ass on this fairy to get an audience with the Council, then I would.

"You do understand the Council isn't in session right now? They come together twice a week." Her tone was so patronizing I wanted to lean over the counter and pinch her thin gossamer wings.

"I do know that, thank you." Because I was technically off duty, I'd had to leave my gun and badge at the office. However, I was still in uniform, and that should have been enough to let the prissy fairy know that I meant business. "I also know that several Council members work here on a day-to-day basis. I don't necessarily need the entire Council. Just one member will do. I have a question that needs answering."

"Maybe I can help you?" She blocked again, and my energy swirled with irritation. As tempting as it was to freeze her and stroll on past, I resisted.

"Above your pay grade, I'm afraid. Please, call whoever is here and let them know I request an urgent audience. I'm sure they know who I am and why I'm here." Folding my arms across my chest and planting my feet firmly on the floor, I let her see I had no intention of moving from this spot until I got what I wanted.

"Fine." She huffed, typing into her screen and then speaking to the hologram that appeared in front of her.

"Sorry to bother you, sir," she breathed, her demeanor different from what she showed me, "but I have Enforcer Black here requesting to speak to a Council member. She says you'll know what it's about."

"I've no clue what she wants, but by all means, show her through," a male voice answered. I couldn't see his image from where I stood, but it didn't matter. I just needed answers from the Council, and this man had them.

"This way."

I followed the receptionist through the security doors and into a passageway with offices branching off both sides. About halfway down, she stopped, knocked on the half-open door, then ushered me inside.

The office was decorated remarkably similar to Director Ridgeway's, all modern glass and sleek lines. Behind the desk sat a huge middle-aged man, his finger idly swirling in a water bowl. I assumed he was a Water Sprite, not only by the bowl of water but also by the room's multiple water features. He got to his feet when I entered and held out his hand.

"Enforcer Black. Please, have a seat. I'm George Kane. What can I do for you today?" I shook his hand but couldn't bring myself to sit down. I was way too agitated. Instead, I stood before his desk, hands clasped behind my back.

"I want to know why the Council insists my species be classified."

George frowned. "Um. I'm not sure what you mean. Are you unclassified?"

"You know I am. Enforcer Raven Black, paranormal of undetermined species. The Council has informed Director Ridgeway that all SIA agents must be species classified to continue working for the agency." My words ran together. I was nervous, as well as angry, and I could feel my power spiraling up inside me. I felt a sizzle at my fingertip as a small spark escaped. I hadn't been this wound up in a long time. I just hoped I could hold myself together and not start levitating things in George's office.

"Who told you this?" George leaned back in his chair, studying me intently.

"Director Ridgeway, sir. I've already undergone a round of painful, invasive tests. I am about to do it all over again, thanks to some malfunction. I want to know why. Why now? Why is it so important the Council knows what species I am?"

"We don't."

"What do you mean?" It was my turn to frown.

"I mean, the Council hasn't issued any such order. If you passed all the testing requirements to enter the SIA, that's good enough for us. We have no interest beyond you doing your job."

I was silent for a minute. "So... you didn't tell the director I need to be classified?"

"No."

My mind whirled, and I plopped into the chair before his desk, at a loss for words. Even though I'd suspected something was up, to have it confirmed rattled me. The Council wasn't behind the sudden interest in my species. Was it the director? Or was someone else pulling her strings?

"I can see you're confused, Enforcer Black, and I concur. If someone is passing on fraudulent orders to the SIA, it needs to be investigated. Especially if it's supposedly coming from the Council."

"You think a Council member has taken it upon themselves to do this?" I was surprised. Council members were heavily vetted and had to be voted in by their respective species. It wasn't easy to get elected.

"It wouldn't be the first time a Council member has overstepped. Probably won't be the last. But rest assured, Enforcer, while your situation is rare, it is of no consequence to us. If and when you find out what you are, by all means, please inform us so your records can be updated, but that is the extent of our interest. And please be assured I'll be investigating this further."

I rose, wiping my palms on my thighs and holding out my hand to shake his. "Thank you so much." I appreciated his honesty and candor.

"Before you go"—George rose again and walked with me to the door—"please don't mention any of this to Director Ridgeway. If the perpetrator of these actions is not this end—it could be someone in the SIA. I'd prefer not to tip them off that we're investigating."

"Right. Of course. I won't say anything."

I left the Council rooms in a daze. Someone, somewhere, had lied. They'd made up the story about the Council changing the rules on classification. But it also meant they knew about me, and for some reason, my species was important to them. My next question was, why? Why would it matter to anyone else what I was?

Arriving home, agitated and confused, I couldn't stop my mind from going around in circles. The medical lab called, but I ignored them. They were expecting me to turn up for testing. That wouldn't be happening. Instead, I changed into my workout gear and went for a run. I needed to burn off some of the energy that was building to powder keg proportions.

SEVENTEEN

The run helped. Calm and in control, I sighed when I rounded the corner and saw Carter leaning against his truck out front of my building, ankles crossed, arms over his chest, cap pulled low over his eyes. I tried to ignore the way my heart skipped a beat at the sight of him.

"Hey." Spotting me, he straightened up and stood on the sidewalk, waiting for me to reach him.

"Hey." I was calmer now, not so angry at myself and what I'd allowed to happen between us, but still mighty pissed about the circumstances around the ordered medical testing.

"What are you doing here?" I stopped a few feet away and did some cooling-down stretches.

"You didn't turn up at medical. I wanted to make sure you were okay."

"I'm fine." I wanted to blurt out what I'd discovered, but suddenly I was unsure of myself with him. I felt a spark of my earlier anger returning. Not at Carter, but at myself. I'd allowed what had happened to happen. Sex, I reminded myself, it was just sex. Yes, but it was sex with Carter, I argued silently. And it was good. More than good, it was beyond anything I'd ever experienced before. And that scared the shit out of me. And made me angry again. Because if sex with him had been awful, I could have pushed it out of my head, argued that we'd tried, but, hey, it didn't work out, no chemistry. Instead, we had chemistry out the wazoo, and that, I hadn't counted on.

"Raven." He shook his head, grinning at me, a dimple flashing. Why did he have to be so damn gorgeous? "You want to talk out here or go inside?"

"I don't think we need to talk at all." That was a big fat lie, but then, I'm big on avoidance. If I could pretend nothing was wrong, that nothing had changed, excellent.

"Fine. Out here it is. Look, what happened today in the parking lot? It was amazing. You were amazing. I know you're freaked out, pissed off, scared. All of those things. I also know you think you can ignore me, and I'll go away, but guess what? That's not going to happen because I'm not going away."

"Only because we work together." I pouted.

"Nope. What happened between us has got nothing to do with work. It's about you and me. You know me, Raven. And I know you."

"It was just sex." I refused to look at him, instead stretching my head to my toes, feeling the pull in my hamstrings. Anything to avoid him and this awful conversation.

"It was so much more than sex, and that's what's got you running scared."

Christ, it was as if he was in my head. And that pissed me off even more. Straightening up, I headed inside. If I was fast enough, I could get into the elevator and up to my apartment without him.

I wasn't quick enough. He slid into the elevator right behind me. Who was I kidding? I knew he would.

"I do have regrets, you know." He leaned against the elevator wall, watching me. I cast a sideways glance at him. "I regret our first time was up against a car. That it was fast and furious when what I really want, what I've thought about way too frequently to be healthy, is a slow burn. To have you naked beneath me, to touch and explore every inch of you, to have you shatter in my arms over and over again."

I gulped. His words turned me on, the picture they painted in my mind an instant aphrodisiac. Now that he'd voiced them, I wanted that too. And just like that, I was on him. My mouth ground down on his, a mash of teeth and tongues, my hands all over him, tugging his shirt free from his pants and exploring the flesh beneath. Somewhere, a dim alarm was ringing in the back of my mind. This wasn't smart. I'd told myself I wouldn't do this again. But I wanted more. I couldn't help myself. Now that I'd tasted Alex Carter, I craved him. More of him. All of him. It sobered me, and I wrenched myself out of his arms and plastered myself to the opposite side of the elevator. I was dragging in deep, gasping breaths when the elevator dinged and deposited us outside my apartment.

The silence between us was electric as he shadowed me to my doorstep, his presence a tangible pressure against my back. My key trembled in the lock, betraying my inner turmoil. Once inside, Carter closed the door with a soft click and paused, a silent question hanging in the air.

I approached him, the mere inches between us

charged with the energy of a brewing storm. I tipped my head back to meet his gaze. "What do you want from me?"

"Everything." His answer was a whisper against my lips before they met in a kiss that spoke of raw need and aching tenderness. His hands were gentle as they helped me shed my shirt, his touch igniting sparks along my skin. We were a tangle of limbs and breaths as we stripped away the last of our clothes, a dance of urgency and desire.

He lifted me then, a fluid motion that spoke of strength and certainty, and I found myself on the bed, my heart racing. The heat in Carter's eyes promised a different tempo this time—a slow burn rather than a wild blaze.

He descended, his lips grazing my cheek, a whisper of a kiss that teased and taunted. I sought his mouth, needing the anchor of his kiss, but he evaded with a low chuckle. Frustration melted into a gasp as his lips found new territory to claim, marking a trail of heat down my neck. His hands were both worship and torment on my skin, drawing forth cries that were half-plea, half-acclamation.

"You taste so good," he murmured, his voice rough with desire, promising more sweet discoveries. His descent was a journey of anticipation, each breath a note in the symphony of our coupling.

And when he reached the core of my being, the world narrowed to the point of his touch. The crescendo built within me, wave upon wave, until it broke over me, leaving me adrift in a sea of sensation. His name was a litany on my lips as the tide of warmth rolled through me, relentless and exquisite.

When he positioned himself, our joining was a homecoming, a perfect melding of two halves into a whole. Our movements were a shared rhythm, a pulsing beat that drove us to the edge and beyond. My whispers became cries, urging him on, and he met each call with a deeper claim.

The world splintered into a thousand stars as we found our release together, a single entity forged in the fire of our passion. In the aftermath, I floated, utterly transformed, every part of me imprinted with his essence.

This was more than physical—this was a confluence of souls, a testament to a connection that defied the ordinary. With Carter, I was more myself than I had ever been, and I knew nothing would ever be the same again.

"Uh, babe?" He'd collapsed on top of me, and I welcomed his weight. My legs had shifted to wrap loosely around the back of his thighs, holding him against me, unwilling to let go, not just yet.

"Mmmmm?" I still wasn't sure I could form coherent words. I was adrift in the afterglow, content, and sated.

"You do know we're floating, right?" His mouth was against my ear, and I shivered at the warmth of his breath. Then, his words penetrated. Floating? My eyes sprang open, and I saw the ceiling, literally two feet from my face.

"What?" I squeaked, and we started to drop rapidly.

"Don't drop us!" Carter growled as I felt him tense around me. Regaining control of my levitation skills, I slowed our rapid descent.

"That was different." I chuckled, the mattress once again firm beneath my back. Carter rolled to my side, tucking me close, my head on his shoulder.

"That happen often?" There was an edge to his voice, and I could practically feel the jealousy rolling off him. He knew I'd had other lovers in the past, but now was certainly not the time to talk about them. Even I had more sense than that.

"Never." But it didn't hurt to reassure him that

never had I never levitated from my bed in the throes of passion before. His jealousy receded as quickly as it came, in its place, a sense of smugness, and I let myself laugh. Boys and their egos. Lying in the afterglow, I couldn't stop thinking about Carter and me and our undeniable chemistry. And my feelings for him. As much as I'd been running from them for so long, I knew the time had come to stop.

Propping myself up on one elbow, I looked down at him. "I don't let people in. It's not who I am. It's not who I raised myself to be." My pause was fraught with emotion. "But I let you in."

"It must be scary." He brushed my hair back over my shoulder and caressed my cheek.

"You have no idea how scared I am," I admitted, turning my face to kiss his palm, "but I'm also excited. I know you have this unwavering faith that this"—I indicated the two of us—"is the right thing that we're meant to be. And maybe..."

"Maybe?" His voice was deep and low, and a shiver ran up my spine, a delightful, full-of-anticipation-and-lust shiver.

"Maybe you're right," I whispered, drowning in his eyes.

"I'll take it." Cupping his hand around my neck,

he tugged me down, kissing me with an intensity that took my breath away. Again.

Banging on my front door woke me from the deep, dreamless sleep I'd fallen into, wrapped in Carter's arms. Untangling myself, I slid out of bed, slipped on a pair of panties and a tank, and silently made my way downstairs. The banging had stopped momentarily. I stood on tiptoes and peeked through the viewfinder to discover Nate Wilder standing at my door, raising his fist to begin banging again.

Flicking the locks, I flung the door open.

"What do you want, and what did you bring me for breakfast?" I demanded. Hands on hips, I eyed the handsome vampire. In the back of my mind, I lamented the fact that as hot as Nate was when he'd kissed me, we'd had zero chemistry. I didn't have the urge to rip his clothes off and ravish him. If I had, maybe I wouldn't be in the predicament I was with Carter right now.

"Didn't know it was a requirement." Nate brushed past me without waiting for an invitation, flopping down onto the sofa with an air of relaxed ease.

"What are you doing here? And how did you even get past the front entrance?" Damn it, this building was meant to be secure. I couldn't have every Tom, Dick, and Paranormal turning up on my doorstep whenever they pleased.

"A bit of persuasion took care of that." Nate winked, and I guessed he'd compelled one of my neighbors to let him in.

"Turning up here isn't smart," I told him, standing by the door, hoping he'd see sense and leave. "The SIA has a warrant out for your arrest. I'm obliged to take you in."

"I'd like to see you try," Nate drawled, his voice thick with innuendo. "I mean, really, I'd like it. Especially in that outfit." He dragged his eyes over my legs, and I remembered I was standing in my underwear. Of course, that was the precise moment Carter appeared at the top of the stairs.

"What the fuck?" he growled, pounding downstairs. He'd pulled his pants on, but his feet were bare, and his shirt unbuttoned, revealing tantalizing glimpses of his chest.

Nate looked from me to Carter and back again, a brow arching and a sly grin creeping across his face.

"Well, well, well," he drawled. "The little anomaly and the wolf finally getting it on."

"None of your business, Nate." I snapped my attention back to him and tried to ignore Carter, who'd crossed to me and stood in front of me as if to protect me from Nate. As if I needed protecting. I shoved him in the back. "Get out of the way."

"He could be dangerous," Carter protested, body rigid, alert for trouble.

"Two things." I blew out an exasperated breath. "One, does he look like he's here to hurt me?" I waved a hand at Nate's sprawled position on my sofa. "And second, I'm a trained SIA agent with kick-ass paranormal powers. I can take care of myself. I don't need you or anyone else protecting me."

"She's perfectly safe with me." The look Nate gave me could only be described as wicked. "I could—"

"Shut your mouth." Carter cut him off, his growl low and deep. I felt it vibrate through the floor.

"I'm just saying..." Nate rose to his feet, and I tensed. The testosterone in the room was so thick I could choke on it.

"You don't get to say anything. Not about her."

"Dude. I can rock her world, and she knows it."

"Oh yeah? Her world got rocked plenty last night, thanks. Three times, in fact."

"Er, guys?" I broke in. This was getting

ridiculous. And I was still standing here in my underwear while they stood chest to chest in a stupid male pissing contest.

"Just three? Oh, I'm so sorry, sweetheart," Nate said. The moment Carter's fist met Nate's jaw, it wasn't just bone that felt the impact—it was the air itself, crackling with the kind of electric fury that promised thunderstorms. Nate reeled, the sharp twist of his face more than just flesh and bone bending—it was the ripple of a reality disrupted, a human facade flickering to reveal the beast beneath.

Nate recovered, his fist coming up in a blur that whispered of dark alleys and darker magic. His punch sliced the air, aiming for Carter, who deftly avoided it.

They clashed, a symphony of snarls and grunts, two forces of nature disguised in human skin. My living room transformed into their battleground, and with a sigh, I turned my back on the two idiots and headed upstairs to get dressed. I wasn't interested in all this male power play bullshit, but when I heard my coffee table break, well, let's say I reached my breaking point. Stopping on the landing, I flung out my hands, freezing them both in place.

"Seriously, boys?" I shouted at them. "You two

want to bash the living shit out of each other, don't do it here. This is my home. Morons."

I left them frozen, unable to move or speak, suspended with Carter's hand wrapped around Nate's neck. I wasn't concerned for the vampire. After all, he didn't actually need to breathe, so while being frozen with your windpipe crushed in someone's hand wasn't ideal, he wouldn't die. Carter, however, was probably going to be pissed with me since Nate's booted foot had just connected with his crotch, and that had to hurt.

Maybe they'd both learn a lesson from this. Grabbing a pair of jeans, fresh underwear, and a T-shirt, I took a shower, dressed, and finally returned to the living room twenty minutes later. With a wave of my hand, I released Nate and Carter. Both men staggered away from each other, Nate clasping his throat, Carter clasping his groin.

"Finished?" I asked, eyeing them both. Nate nodded, whispered a strangled "sorry" through his damaged windpipe, while Carter looked at me with watery eyes, falling to his knees and trying to hide his pain.

"Coffee, anyone?" I asked conversationally, wandering into the kitchen and flicking the coffee machine on. While it was warming up, I opened the freezer and took out a popsicle, throwing it at Carter, who caught it with one hand. "For your..." I nodded at his crotch. "I don't have a cold pack or bag of peas. That'll have to do." I bit my lips to stop laughing as I watched him gingerly place the popsicle on the front of his pants.

"I apologize." Nate's voice was back to normal, his superhuman healing powers at work. "I'll pay for the damage."

"Yes, you will," I agreed. The coffee table was toast, smashed to pieces, and two holes were in my wall. Nate straightened the overturned furniture and returned the books that had fallen from the bookcase. Carter crawled onto an armchair and remained there with the popsicle in his lap.

Fixing three cups of coffee, I handed one to Nate and Carter and cradled my own between my hands. I took the armchair opposite Carter and pointed to the sofa. "Sit," I told Nate. He sat.

"Now, Nate," I began, "before we take a trip downtown"—I held up my hand to stop him when he would have protested—"Why are you here?"

"You asked Ethan to go through the footage from the club, isolate the patrons who'd been there the same nights as the victims."

"I did. I take it he found something?" I shouldn't

be surprised that Ethan had gone to Nate with his discovery first.

"As you'd expect, there are several people who are regulars at the club, but there was one that stood out."

"Oh?"

Carter leaned forward, elbows on his knees, his expression intent.

"Vince Santiago." Pulling out his phone, Nate pulled up a photo. Vince Santiago was a big man, balding, mean-looking. "I came across him years ago, right after he turned. We had a disagreement when I freed the women he was keeping as blood slaves. Vince is a career criminal. A thug. In and out of prison when he was human—he's violent, a murderer and rapist."

"Great. And now he's a vampire. Those traits will only be amplified."

"Correct. I don't know what he's doing in Redmeadows, but considering he frequented my club on the nights your victims were there, I'd say it's beyond coincidence."

"Who turned him?" I asked. "Are they here, giving him instructions?"

"Ha!" Nate snorted. "From what I know, he was turned when the drug and prostitution gang he was recruiting for kidnapped a vampire's blood donor. Said vampire turned up to reclaim his property and killed the entire gang; only Vince didn't die. He turned."

"But isn't he sired to the one who turned him?"

"Not if that vampire denies you. Then you're on your own."

"A rogue," I muttered.

"Your specialty, I believe."

"We need to bring him in," Carter said. He had pulled up Vince's record on his phone. "This guy is a piece of work. We don't want his sort in Redmeadows. He's got form, back when he was human with the drug, prostitution, and human trafficking rings. Not a stretch to think he'd dabble in kidnapping humans and auctioning them off to the highest bidder."

I turned to Nate. "Do you think he has the smarts to orchestrate this? Or is he working for someone else?"

"Oh, I think he is more than capable of pulling this off." Nate sat back, seeming satisfied with what he'd told us. "And now I really should be going. Dawn isn't far off."

Locking the door behind him, I turned to look at Carter, who was sitting much more comfortably.

"So, do we take this bit of news to the director? She'll be pissed we didn't bring Wilder in," Carter said.

"I don't want to tell her." I shook my head. "There's something I discovered yesterday that I haven't told you yet."

"Oh?"

"Instead of going to medical, I went to see the Council."

"What?" He bolted up, crossing to me and grasping my shoulders. "That was ballsy. Why? To tear them a new one for making you go through the tests in the first place?"

"Pretty much. But here's the thing. I spoke with Councilor Kane, who told me the Council didn't order anything. They don't care. They have zero interest in my species, and as long as I'm doing my job and obeying the law, that's all they care about."

Carter was silent, digesting my words. "So you think, what? Someone in the SIA is behind it?"

"Either someone in the SIA or a counselor abusing their position and sending fraudulent orders to the SIA."

"But you think Director Ridgeway is involved?"

I nodded. "The couple of times I've spoken with her about it, something was a little off. Now that I know the Council did not order my classification as a priority—in fact, not at all—her behavior toward me? Suspicious."

"Okay. So we think she's involved. The next question is, why? Why does she care what you are? What difference does it make?" I loved how he believed me straight away, that he was immediately on my side. My heart softened even more. Alex Carter was well and truly under my skin.

"That's the part that doesn't make any sense. I've no idea. But in the meantime, while I'm trying to figure it out, I want to give her a wide berth. Let's bring Vince Santiago in for questioning. She'll find out after the fact."

Vince Santiago was a difficult vampire to find. He was an expert in covering his tracks, and so far, we had no leads except for Crimson Mist nightclub. But even then, if Vince was behind the abductions, he wasn't taking patrons from the club. Maybe that was where he targeted them, snatching them later. The trouble was, it was all guesswork until we got the man himself into an interview room.

To complicate things further, word had gotten back to Carter's pack about our relationship. My stomach still clenched at the word, at the thought of what it meant. *A relationship? Me? Am I insane?* But I couldn't deny the way I felt about Carter, and once that door was opened, there was no closing it. I'd wanted no-strings sex. He was happy to provide the sex, but he'd made it clear that for him, there would always be strings. And now I was starting to feel that way too, curious about what we could be together. And it scared the ever-living daylights out of me. I didn't need the added pressure of his pack, and I wondered how they found out. I hadn't told anyone about us, but maybe Carter had. It wasn't like it was a secret, but I wasn't shouting it from the rooftops either.

My biggest worry? He'd realize he'd made a colossal mistake in being with me, that I'm damaged, incapable of love. Eventually, it would wear him down, and he'd walk away, but we'd be forced to see and work with each other daily. My chest ached at the thought.

"You're thinking too hard." Carter had finished the call he'd been on and stepped up to my side, lacing his fingers with mine. I glanced down at our clasped hands and couldn't help the involuntary curve of my lips. I liked holding hands with him. I liked touching him. I liked him altogether too much.

"Was that your pack?" I nodded at the phone he'd shoved into the back pocket of his jeans.

"Don't worry about them." He brought our clasped hands up and kissed the back of my hand.

"Carter." I sighed, pulling us both to a stop. "Did you just bail on the pack?"

"No. I simply refused their invitation. I've got plans with you."

Our first official date. Dinner at the Witches Brew. He knew it was my favorite place, that I was comfortable there, and he was going out of his way to make sure I was comfortable, that I didn't bolt.

"Carter, your pack is already wary of me. I've had voicemails from April today asking me to put the pack first and terminate my relationship with you. Which reminds me—how did they find out? Did you tell them?"

"Travis was waiting for me when I got home. He smelt you. All over me. I didn't have to say anything." He resumed walking, tugging me with him. "Look, I'm sorry about the pack bullshit—and that's what it is. They've no business interfering. Ignore them. That's what I'm doing."

"But Carter..." My mind was a whirl with the implications of what this could mean for him. "They're your pack. Your family. You can't turn your back on them."

"I'm not. But I won't have them trying to run my life either. Just because April got it into her head that I'd be a good mate for her cousin Storm doesn't mean she has a say in my love life. I choose you. End of story."

"But you need a wolf to mate with," I whispered, worried about the implications of...everything.

"Nope. I don't. I'm not an Alpha. I'm not obliged to take a wolf as a mate. Naturally, the pack would be ecstatic if I did, but it's not pack law. Plus, they know you, Raven." We'd stopped on the sidewalk again, and he released my hands to cup my shoulders and stare directly into my eyes. "They know you're a good person, and they know you make me happy. They'll come around. I'm not worried, and neither should you be. Now. Can we please just enjoy our date?"

He leaned down and nibbled gently on my lower lip, distracting me from my troubles, which weren't really my troubles. They were his, but the guilt was eating at me until his distraction tactics worked, and I didn't give a flying toss about his pack or anyone else. Pulled tight against him, his mouth ravaging mine; he was all I needed, all I wanted. I contemplated stripping him naked and having my way with him against the restaurant wall when a group of teens walked past, laughing and telling us to get a room. Slowly disengaging, Carter lifted his head, his eyes dark with desire, his breathing heavy.

"We'd better go in before we're arrested," he muttered, adjusting his jeans and taking my hand again.

"Right," I agreed, unable to string together a sentence while my mind was occupied with thoughts of him.

He'd booked ahead, and I could feel all eyes on us as the waitress led us to our table. Not surprising given the display we'd just given them all outside. Pulling out my chair for me, Carter waited until I was seated before taking the seat opposite. I picked up the menu and buried my face in it.

"Are you—nervous?" he asked. I glanced at him over the top of my menu and felt my cheeks heat. I didn't answer; I lifted the menu higher so he couldn't see me.

"I can feel...something coming off you in waves, and it isn't desire. You're nervous." His voice was low, so no one else could hear. "Raven." Plucking the menu from my fingers, he leaned forward, elbows on the table, and studied me intently. I looked away.

"Talk to me." He didn't demand, more like begged, which pulled at my heartstrings. Letting out my breath with a sigh, I gave in, looking him in the eye.

"Yes. I'm nervous. This is my first date."

He nodded. "Our first date."

"Our first date, and my very first date."

"You're...you mean you've never been on a date before? Ever?" Surprise laced his words, and I frowned. I got it; I was twenty-eight years old, and I'd never dated. I was weird. My face grew hotter, and I hated that I was blushing, that he'd easily be able to see the red staining my cheeks thanks to my ultra-pale skin.

"Well,"—he cleared his throat and reached over, brushing his knuckles across my cheek—"I'm honored that your very first date is with me. I'll try and make it a good one."

"Right." Pulling out my phone, I glanced at the time, counting down to when I could leave. This was mortifying.

"No, I mean it, Raven. I'm sorry if I made you uncomfortable. I should have realized. You've told me a million times you don't do relationships. I should have figured out that it meant you didn't go on dates, either. This isn't how I want our date to go, with you feeling uncomfortable and checking the time so you can leave. Please. Put your phone away. I'll order us drinks and let's have a good time, yes? No pressure. Don't think of it as a date. Think of it as hanging out with me. We've had plenty of meals together before. This is no different."

He was right; we had eaten meals together and spent countless hours together in the past. But this time *was* different. Now there were feelings and emotions and expectations, and I didn't know how to deal with any of them. And I was so scared of messing this up. Carter seemed to have every bit of faith that we'd be fine, our relationship was meant to be, but I'd spent so long avoiding it that I couldn't switch gears so quickly.

"Okay. A drink would be good." I smiled, determined to put in the same effort he was.

He ordered us whiskey, and the golden liquid not only warmed my stomach but also soothed my nerves, and I relaxed. Surprise of all surprises, I had a good time. The food was magnificent, the drinks kept coming, and Carter was attentive, funny, and a great conversationalist. He kept me laughing, and I loved him for it. I didn't spare a thought for his pack, what the future held, or try to dissect every word and action.

"Well?" Carter paid the bill, then took my hand once again and led me outside.

"Well, what?" I asked, looking up at the night

sky. It was a clear night, and the stars twinkled brightly.

"As a first date, how would you rank it?" We began moving down the footpath, hands still linked. Releasing him from my grasp, I slid my arm around his waist and leaned into him, smiling when he looped his arm around my shoulders and squeezed.

"I'd say it was pretty good."

"Pretty good? Is that all?" He laughed, and I could feel it rumble through me.

"Well, I have nothing to compare it to, now do I?" I teased. "I'm going to need more dates before I can rank you."

"Ah, I see. Let me assure you, Miss Black, I see many more dates in your future." He spun me in front of him, hands at my waist, and kissed me.

"Ow," I yelped, pushing back from him.

"What happened? Did I hurt you?" he asked, then cursed and jumped back from me. I twisted to look at the back of my leg, where I'd felt a sharp sting. Something had bitten me. Only there was no insect in sight, just a dart protruding from the back of my thigh. I plucked it out and held it in front of me. Then, I noticed an identical dart sticking out of Carter's shoulder. He removed it, and we both looked at each other.

"Shit," we said in unison.

"We've been drugged." He cursed again, shoved the dart into his jacket pocket, and took my hand, hurrying me down the footpath. "We've got to hurry. Try and make it to your apartment before it kicks in. I'd assume it's a sedative by how it was delivered."

"Who?" I puffed, hurrying to keep up with his long strides. Then it hit me. "Stop, Carter! We're exerting ourselves. If our heart rate rises, the sedative will work its way through our system faster. We need to walk, not run, and stay calm."

"Too late." He staggered, and I clutched him, trying to keep my footing. We must've looked like two drunken idiots staggering home after a big night out.

"We can still make it." I gasped, tripping over my own feet. I slowed my steps and tried to keep my breathing even. The horizon blurred before me, and I blinked to clear it. The world tilted on its axis, and I struggled to stay upright. My mind was foggy, and my body heavy.

"Carter..." I couldn't remember what I wanted to say. I could hear him next to me; tried to reach out a hand to him, but I'd lost control of my limbs. I heard footsteps behind me, knew we were in danger, and my adrenaline spiked, giving me a boost. Rounding the corner, I saw my apartment building. It was weaving and swaying in a very unusual way, and I squinted in confusion. A car roared past, then its brakes squealed. Something clattered to the footpath, and I peered down to see my phone. I didn't remember pulling it out of my pocket. Staggering to a halt, I tried to bend down and pick it up, but the sidewalk was dipping and moving, and my phone kept moving out of reach. I collapsed on one knee, putting out a hand to steady myself.

"Alex. I'm in trouble." I saw him fall just in front of me. He'd heard me call him by his first name—something I never did—and he'd turned back to me, only he overbalanced and fell. I had to get us help. We were in big, big trouble. My fingers fumbled and finally closed over the phone. Had I called someone? Was the call still connected? I couldn't think, couldn't focus. My hand flew to the comms unit on my wrist, only it wasn't there. Oh, that's right. I wasn't in uniform. Off duty. On a date. With Carter.

The footsteps were close, almost upon me. I raised my arm and tried to freeze whoever approached, but they kept coming closer and closer. The more I waved my arm, the more off-balance I became until I collapsed on my back, my breath whooshing out. My heartbeat thundered in my ears, my tongue felt swollen in my mouth, and my limbs had all the strength of a limp strand of spaghetti.

Dimly I heard a car reversing, the squeak of brakes followed by a door opening and closing. Then a dark figure standing over me. My fingers twitched, and I tried to summon my power, but nothing happened. Then the figure leaned over me. I tried to focus, to see who it was, but my eyes wouldn't cooperate. Then a sharp sting in my neck. Everything was blurry and heavy, and I knew they'd drugged me even further, that I was well and truly screwed. My only hope was that whoever I'd called had heard me.

I DIDN'T KNOW how long I was out, but when I woke up, I felt like shit. My mouth was dry, my eyes stung, and I had a ripper of a headache. I tried to raise my hand to my face, and that's when I discovered they were tied behind my back. My wriggling fingers brushed against something, and I heard a crinkling sound. Had they wrapped my hands? To stop me from using my power? Letting my head fall back, I glanced around.

I was in a cage. Bigger than the ones we'd found on Wolf Hill. Cleaner too. I was propped up; my legs stretched out in front of me. Looking beyond the cage, I could see old red brick walls on either side and dirty plastic sheeting hung from the ceiling, creating a small room. Besides the cage, there was a gurney, currently unoccupied, a giant lamp, the kind you see in operating theaters, and a trolley that at the moment sat empty.

Carter was out next to me, slumped against the cold metal of his cage. His breathing was even, a sign he was still alive, just knocked out. The drug they'd used was potent, leaving him in a vulnerable quiet that didn't suit him at all. I kept my gaze fixed on the rise and fall of his chest, a silent rhythm in the stark silence of our holding cells. Despite the chill of the steel bars, a kind of heat radiated from my skin—a mix of worry and a growing rage against those who'd put us here.

It didn't take a genius to figure out we'd been taken by the same assholes who'd kidnapped and tortured the humans. Old red dusty bricks. Medical facilities. Well, you could call it a medical facility at a stretch. My best guess, I was in an old warehouse or factory. It was cold and dim, and I couldn't hear any outside noise.

I flexed my power and tried to see if I could use it to free my hands or unlock the cage. Nothing. Not even a tingle. Whoever had done this had worked out a way to neutralize my power. Clever. Not many people knew my hands were the key, and those that did? Worked at the SIA.

A headache pounded relentlessly behind my eyes, and despite my predicament, I gave in and closed them, breathing in slow deep breaths to ease the pain. I must have dozed off because the next time I awoke, a man was standing in front of my cage, the big medical lamp now ablaze and silhouetting him so I couldn't make out his features.

"Sleeping beauty awakes." I didn't recognize the voice.

"Who are you?" I tried to see, but all I got was a vague outline. He stepped forward, a baseball bat in one hand, resting on his shoulder. Approaching the cage, he stopped, giving me a good look at him.

"Vince Santiago," I muttered. Should have known.

"At your service." He brought the baseball bat down, slapping it against his hand threateningly. I wasn't sure I liked where this was going.

"Heard you've been looking for me." He wasn't tall, five foot ten at the most, but he was a big man.

Broad-shouldered and, despite his overweight gut, I could see he had strength. He had tattoos on the back of both hands and scars on his face. He smelled of stale smoke and blood. He might have turned at forty-six, but he looked at least ten years older.

"Word travels fast." Considering Carter and I had only started searching for him today, we'd obviously come close for word to reach him so quickly.

Suddenly he swung the baseball bat, and I flinched when it hit the side of the cage with a loud clang. I summoned my power and flung it at him, doing my best to freeze him in place, but nothing happened. Whatever they had encased my hands in had successfully dampened my magic field.

"I was coming for you anyway," he drawled. Leaning forward, he flicked the lock on the cage door, reached in, and dragged me out. Clenching my nape in his hand, he moved his face close to mine, his rancid breath blowing hot and wet over my skin.

I tried not to gag. "Oh?"

"You just moved up the timeline with your nosy questions. No matter. You're here now. Let the fun begin!" He laughed. The asshole actually laughed. Releasing his grip on my neck, he swung the baseball bat again. This time it connected with my stomach, winding me. I gasped and coughed, trying to catch my breath, trying to breathe through the pain. It hurt like the devil, but I was pretty sure nothing was broken. He'd nailed me across the softness of my abdomen. If he'd hit higher up, he'd undoubtedly have smashed a couple of ribs.

Even though Nate had told me what an evil bastard Vince was, I hadn't expected what followed. The beating went on for what felt like forever, blow after blow, all over my body. Bones broke, skin split, and I was in a world of pain, delirious with it. I prayed for oblivion, for him to deliver a blow to my head that would end it all, for I couldn't escape. I fell. Unable to keep my balance or break my fall, I smacked my head hard into the concrete floor, but he didn't let that deter him. He kicked me in the back, rolling me with his boot, and then beat me unmercifully with the bat.

I thought I heard Carter, thought I heard him roar, fight to get out of his cage, but I couldn't be sure.

Vince seemed to enjoy my screams, but eventually, they died down. My body was limp as he swung at me with the bat. I was nothing. Broken and empty and praying for death, my mind left my body at the pain it was enduring. Instead, I let myself drift, let myself revisit memories of things that made me happy. Carter. My sorrow at his devastation when I die. I prayed he was still out of it and not witness to what Vince had done to me. That the growls and snarls I thought I'd heard weren't from him. I prayed the same fate wasn't awaiting him. I couldn't stand to know he might go through the same thing. Drugged and powerless, beaten to death by a sadistic bastard we'd underestimated.

"Jesus, Vince!" A woman's voice registered on the edge of my consciousness. "What the fuck have you done? I need her alive, damn you."

I couldn't open my eyes; they were swollen shut.

"She is," he protested.

"Barely." There was something familiar about the voice, but I couldn't focus, couldn't concentrate beyond the pain I was in. "Get away from her, you moron. If she dies, you die with her."

"You've got balls, lady." Vince laughed. "No one threatens me and gets away with it." Sounds of a scuffle reached my ears, the familiar whoosh of the baseball bat, and I couldn't help but flinch as I waited for impact. Only it didn't land on me. Instead, there was a loud clang as it hit the floor, then the sharp crack of a gunshot, followed by the sound of a body hitting the ground. Had the woman shot him? Didn't she know you couldn't kill a vampire by shooting it? A stake through the heart or decapitation was the only way.

"Damn," she was muttering, I could barely hear her, but I sensed she was close to my side; wished I was able to open my eyes. "Hold on. Don't you fucking die. I need you." I figured she was talking to herself more than me because I was in no shape to answer her. I guessed I was pretty horrific to look at.

"Morphine. For the pain." A sting in my arm, mild compared to what I'd endured so far, then the bliss of the painkilling drug as it flooded my system, easing the pain, dulling everything, including my mind. I struggled to stay awake, wanted to know who she was, and if they hadn't brought me here to kill me, why bring me here at all? And what about Carter?

NINETEEN

"She's totally healed. Amazing." A man's voice next to me had me popping my eyes open. I was in the red brick warehouse, this time strapped to the gurney, a drip attached to my arm. There was more equipment in the room now, what looked like fridges and workbenches with a barrage of test tubes neatly lined up. My eyes landed on the person the man was talking to. A woman in crisp black pants, a white blouse, red stilettos, and bright red hair cut in a bob. I blinked a couple of times as I digested what I was seeing. Director Ridgeway. It was Director Ridgeway, and although a mask covered her nose and mouth, I still recognized her vivid green eyes and bright red hair.

I quickly closed my eyes again, not wanting

them to know I was awake. I listened to their conversation.

"Remarkable," Director Ridgeway breathed, her voice full of—was that anticipation? She sounded excited. That I'd healed? For I was sure I had. I felt fine, no pain, no foggy brain.

"She self-combusted." He said, voice high with excitement, "Before I could grab the fire extinguisher, the flames had subsided, and her injuries healed."

"Yet she hasn't woken up?"

"I would say she's in some sort of self-induced coma, her mind shutting down while she got to the business of healing herself."

"But she hasn't healed in the same way a vampire would? Or a werewolf?" the director asked.

"No. Definitely a different healing process."

"Interesting." I could hear the director pacing, her heels clicking on the warehouse floor. "The odd occasion she was injured at the SIA, she showed no such abilities."

"Maybe it was latent? Maybe it only works when she's close to death? Could she be a phoenix?" He sounded hopeful.

"An interesting idea, but doubtful. A phoenix can rise again after death. I'm not sure they have these healing abilities. And healing abilities are good. It means we can keep her here indefinitely. If my hunch is correct, she could be the key."

"Indefinitely?" The man's voice went up an octave or two. "But they'll be looking for her."

"I've taken care of that. There was an explosion. Her phone and torn and bloodied clothing were found at the scene. Damaged by the fire but vital evidence that SIA Enforcer Raven Black was killed when a faulty fuel line in her vehicle exploded."

I held my breath, frozen in shock. They'd staged my death? Blew up my car? Lying on the gurney, I could feel I wasn't constricted by clothes. Instead, I was in some sort of hospital gown. My hands were shackled to the side of the gurney, still encased in something. Cracking an eye open, I took a peek. Ah. Silver bags duct-taped around my wrists. Odd, though, that silver had never incapacitated me before.

"How long have you been awake?" I glanced up at the director, who was now standing by my side.

"Not long." I tugged at my restraints. Nope, they weren't budging.

She studied me in silence for a moment longer, then turned to the man behind her. "Begin. The specimen is ready and waiting."

"Yes, ma'am." His words were directed at her departing back. She pushed through the plastic hanging from the ceiling, and I caught a glimpse of another room, similar to mine, divided only by the opaque plastic. I could just make out another gurney and the unmistakable outline of a pair of jean-encased legs strapped down by the ankles. It had to be Carter, strapped down, waiting for...what?

"What's going on here?" I asked the man in the lab coat, who was now jabbing a needle into the vein inside my elbow.

"Nothing for you to concern yourself with," he responded, attaching a plastic tube to the end of the needle and hooking an empty bag to the edge of my gurney. Collecting my blood, and by the looks of things, they intended to collect a lot.

"Considering it looks like you're getting ready to *harvest me*, I'd say it does concern me." I'd chosen the word harvest because I'd seen what was on the trolley by his side. Bone saws. Scalpels. Instruments that made you wince just looking at them. They didn't want only my blood—they wanted all of me.

The director's earlier words came back to me. They'd staged my death, made it look like I'd been blown to pieces. No one would be looking for me. What about Carter? Had they staged his death too?

Or did they have something different planned for him? I felt my eyes well up and quickly blinked to clear them. Now was not the time to get emotional. If I lay here much longer, I'd be too weak to do anything. Carter hadn't moved, not so much as a twitch, so I figured they'd kept him drugged. It was up to me to save both of us.

"Why is she doing this?" I tried again, but the man ignored me. Turning to the fridge, he removed two vials, one containing a clear liquid, the other a yellow liquid.

"What are they?"

He answered without thinking, "One is vampire venom, the other werewolf venom." Carrying them over to an empty trolley, he set the vials in a holder and retrieved three syringes from the drawer.

"Are you going to inject them into me?"

He shook his head. "Not you, no." Placing the syringes on the trolley, he snapped on latex gloves and then looked at me.

"Do you know what species you are?" His voice indicated he was truly curious. I couldn't detect any malice in his tone. This guy was a doctor or scientist, or both.

"No," but something had sparked when I'd woken and heard them discussing me, how I'd self-combusted to heal. I'd read a case like that. A family of fire demons living out in Maxxan, Texas. I couldn't remember the exact details, but I had vague recollections of an old report, long before the official formation of the Supernatural Investigation Agency, detailing something along the lines of a fire demon exiled from his realm due to his relationship with a human. And now I couldn't help but wonder if I was descended from his lineage. I'd need to explore further; I didn't know if I was a fire demon at all. Regardless, I wouldn't reveal that little bit of info to this nutjob. Crossing to my gurney, he reached over and pulled a strap tight across my ribs, just beneath my breasts, then another across my hips and thighs. This couldn't be good.

He glanced down at the floor, moved his foot, and then the bed began to move. I couldn't help the squeak of surprise.

"I need to access your back. This is the easiest way," he explained, keeping his foot on the pedal until I was fully vertical. "Oh, I forgot to secure your head." Next thing, he dragged a footstool over, stood on it, then pulled straps across my forehead, effectively stopping my head from any movement. My position was uncomfortable, suspended vertically, unable to support my weight but held in place by the straps across the gurney that were now cutting into me under the strain.

His foot moved, and he stepped on another pedal, and this time the gurney turned away from him. I could no longer see him or his equipment. I was facing a brick wall. There was a metal sliding noise at my back, then the sound of something on wheels being dragged across the floor, followed by the swab of something cold on my skin.

"What are you doing?" I kept my tone calm, even though my fists were clenching and unclenching in their silver bags as I flexed my power, trying to break free.

"Prepping you for a spinal tap," he absentmindedly answered me.

"Why?" I felt the needle pierce my skin, then the punch as it entered my spinal column. Son of a bitch, it hurt, and I closed my eyes as I sucked in a breath. I'd had this done before, at the SIA medical unit, as part of my testing.

"Need more. Used up all of your first samples on testing. Now I think I've got it, though," he muttered. My suspicions were correct. My initial samples at the medical unit hadn't been ruined by faulty refrigeration. They'd been stolen.

"Got it?"

"The formula. Got to make sure the formula is right, the quantities are right, or it doesn't work. Can't have another failure."

"Formula for what?"

"A hybrid. A super paranormal." I doubted he noticed he was answering my questions. He was so busy with what he was doing, removing the needle from my spine and puttering around behind me, that his mind was responding to me on a different level, a subconscious level.

"Why do we need a hybrid of different species?"

"We don't. Ridgeway does. Wants to build an army, overthrow the Council, and then the humans. Take control."

"Are you done with my back? Can you lower me, do you think? I'm dizzy." It was true. I was feeling light-headed and nauseous.

The bed whirred, returning to its original position and lowering until I was again horizontal. The relief was instantaneous. "Thank you," I muttered. He ignored me, and I lapsed into silence, trying to devise an ingenious plan to get myself out of this predicament. Unfortunately, nothing was forthcoming, and with blood loss making me weak and a headache starting to gather from the spinal tap, I wasn't in much of a condition to do anything. I prayed my newfound healing powers weren't a one-off.

Instead, I thought about the director's plan. That's why the victims we'd found had multiple DNA in their bodies. She'd been injecting them with vampire and werewolf serum, hoping to create some hybrid creature. Clearly, her plan hadn't worked; we'd seen that with four of her victims. Why would my DNA make a difference? Had she tried other paranormal creatures as well? Fae? Dragons? Although good luck capturing a dragon and then getting its DNA.

I watched as the man placed a vial of what I assumed was my spinal fluid into a machine, closed the lid, and pressed some buttons. The machine started up with a whir and began vibrating. Then he moved over and opened a laptop, and began typing furiously.

Closing my eyes on the exhaustion creeping up, I let my thoughts drift, trying to remember what I'd learned about the realm where fire demons lived. I struggled to recall what I knew about them. They were almost a lost race, close to extinction. We'd touched on them briefly during SIA training, but there weren't many of them around. There was the family living in Maxxan, but they had bred with humans, and their DNA diluted. Is that what happened to me? That somewhere along the line, my fire demon DNA had become so diluted it was impossible to identify my species? What were their powers, though? Come on, remember, remember.

Fire magic, obviously. Healing. Peacekeepers. I snickered quietly. Yeah, made sense. I was a Supernatural Investigation Agency Enforcer. A peacekeeper indeed. But I'd never shown any affinity or ability related to fire. And yet Ridgeway and the doc had said I'd self-combusted. Perhaps what they'd said was true, that my real power had only just awakened because I'd been close to death? So, my abilities to freeze and levitate were nothing compared to what I was truly capable of. But what was I truly capable of? And how did I do it?

"Can I have some water?" My mouth was dry, and the strap holding my head in place was too tight.

The scientist swiveled on his chair and looked at me, assessing, then nodded to himself. Opening a fridge, he withdrew a bottle of water. He released the strap around my head and adjusted the bed, so I was on a slight incline. Twisting the lid off the water bottle, he held it to my lips, and I gulped thirstily.

When I drank my fill, I finally pulled away and gave him a nod. "Thank you."

He returned to his laptop without a word and resumed typing. My thoughts wandered again, and I absently gazed at the red brick wall. I thought of my dormant magic and wondered how to use it. What if I built a wall of flames? Built a wall around Carter so they couldn't touch him, for I was very concerned they were about to inject him with the concoction the doctor was creating. Or, if I could get my hands free, I could levitate him out of reach. And freeze Dr. Frankenstein here. The trick would be to keep Carter and me from being burned.

As the thoughts percolated through my mind, something strange happened. A flame appeared, small to begin with, then growing, flickering silently as it danced up to the ceiling, then curved around, enclosing us. It wasn't until the intense heat from the flames finally penetrated the doctor's focus that he looked up.

"What the hell?" He stood, the chair rolling away from him snagged on something, and tipped over. Rushing to the fire extinguisher sitting a few feet away, he hefted it up and sprayed at the fire.

"What did you do?" he accused, glancing at me over his shoulder before turning his attention back to the wall of flame, sweat running down his face. I shrugged. I didn't know what I did. I just thought of a wall of fire, and one appeared. Despite the headache pounding at my temples and the dizzy sensation from blood loss, I seized on that realization. What if it was as simple as thinking things into reality? With nothing to lose, I closed my eyes and concentrated on the straps holding me in place. I visualized fire burning through the leather, of them falling away.

Opening my eyes, I peered down, watching in wonder as the straps lay sizzling on the ground, smoke rising from their scorched remains, yet I was unharmed. The fire hadn't burned me. I spared a thought for my hands, trapped in the silver bags, and before my eyes, the bags exploded into flame. The scientist was still at the wall of fire, the extinguisher making no progress. He was paying no attention to me, which was a good thing. But just in case, I waved a hand and froze him in place, exerting enough pressure to keep him silent but still allowing him to breathe.

Sitting upright, I pulled the needle from my arm and pressed against the wound. I didn't know how my fire demon healing powers worked, but I needed them to work fast. Sitting up had made the room spin, and I didn't have time to hang around and wait. I needed to leave here before the director returned and discovered my little trick.

Sliding off the gurney, I grabbed the bottle of water left on the benchtop and gulped down the remainder of its contents while I thought about my options. I had to destroy this place. I had to make sure they had nothing of my DNA here, and the best way I knew how was fire. But I didn't want to barbecue the doctor. He was my witness against the director.

Cocking my head, I considered the wall of flames, concentrated on manipulating the fire to create an opening, amazed when the fire responded, creating an arch for me to step through. On the other side, I looked down at myself. Not a mark on me, not a blister, not a singed hair. With a grin, I headed to the door, cracked it open, and peered outside. No guards. No one was around. All I could hear was Carter's breathing, deep and even, and the crackle of flames. I pushed through the plastic and approached him. He was restrained like I was and hooked up to an IV, a clear liquid pumping into his veins. Keeping him sedated, I guessed. Freeing him from the restraints, I removed the IV and ran my eyes over him, looking for injury. Nothing was apparent. It seemed Vince hadn't had the chance to attack Carter with the baseball bat. Tugging his limp body into a sitting position, I draped him over my shoulder in a fireman's hold and, with a grunt, lifted him, taking his full weight.

Returning to the doctor, I adjusted my magic and used an invisible leash to drag him toward me. It was an effort, both mentally and physically, to bring them both with me, but I couldn't leave them behind. Crossing the warehouse floor to the far side, I paused beside a filthy window and peeked outside. It was dark, and I couldn't see much. I spotted a vehicle some distance away and wondered if it belonged to the doctor or if someone else was there. I thought it strange the director didn't have the place heavily guarded. If she'd gone to all this trouble to conduct her experiments, surely she'd keep her investment protected?

I wasn't sure if I willed it into existence with my newfound power or if it was just a coincidence, but at that moment, a minivan pulled up outside, and six armed men climbed out, heading for the warehouse. Damn it. I couldn't hold the doctor captive for much longer or support Carter's dead weight over my shoulder. I was still weak. And I needed to keep some of my energy for directing the fire to wipe this place out.

Again, as if the mere thought of it triggered it, a fireball erupted behind me, the gurneys and science lab exploding into flames.

"Shit!" With a squeak, I dashed sideways, pulling up a shield to protect us from the blast. It barely held as the giant fireball barreled across the warehouse, rolled up the shield, and to the roof. The rafter caught fire, and judging by this place's condition, the whole building would be ablaze within minutes. We had to get out. Now.

Releasing the doctor from my hold, I grabbed him by the arm and looked into his eyes. "You'll have to do as I say if you don't want to die. Understand?" My voice was a snarl, threatening all sorts of pain if he tried to run. He nodded, his eyes round with fear as the fire raged around us. We had one shot at this.

"Move. That way, toward the window." I nodded further along the warehouse to a broken window. Over the crackle of the fire, I heard the guards shouting on the opposite side of the warehouse.

"Climb out. Then take him." I sagged against the wall, Carter's dead weight pulling on me. I had to trust the doctor wouldn't run, that he'd help us. I listened as he scrambled up and out the window. I could hear shouting, but the smoke was so thick I couldn't see anything. Which meant they couldn't see us. As far as they knew, all three of us were trapped in the blaze.

"Pass him up." The doctor appeared at the window, and I shoved Carter at him, pushing his legs through and heaving myself up and over behind him. We landed together in a pile of arms and legs. Bruised and shaken but still alive.

TWENTY

The doctor had fallen backward, Carter landing on top of him, still unconscious, his weight pinning him to the ground. I left him there while I sat and caught my breath, dragging in deep gulps of fresh air. Above my head, black smoke billowed from the broken window. Although it was dark outside, it wouldn't be long before the blaze was spotted and the authorities arrived. I hoped.

My throat hurt, and my eyes burned, and I was as weak as a newborn. Yet, I found enough energy to form a snare around the doctor's ankle and tether him to the ground when he wriggled out from beneath Carter. He pulled at the invisible binding holding him captive, but he was stuck fast.

"Check on him." I coughed, voice raw. He looked at me, then nodded, his face blackened by soot, and I imagined I looked the same. Rolling Carter onto his back, he pressed his fingers against his neck, checking his pulse. His face was relatively clean, and I suspected having his face pressed against my back protected his airways significantly.

"He's fine. Still sedated. Pulse strong, breathing okay." He tugged at his ankle again, and my magic stretched and twanged from pulling taut. I couldn't hold him for much longer, I was spent, but there was no need for him to know that.

"Sit down and stop struggling, or I'll freeze all of you, not just your foot," I grumbled. Surprisingly, he did, settling onto his backside and drawing his knees up, resting his arms and head on them.

Leaning back against the warehouse, I pondered my next move when a vehicle tore in and skidded to a halt, its headlights briefly flashing over us before being extinguished. The light momentarily blinded me, and I raised a hand to shield my eyes, but by then, it was dark again, and now I couldn't see a thing.

"Raven?" Footsteps ran toward me.

"Nate?" What was he doing here?

"Are you okay? Are you hurt?" He slid onto his knees by my side, a puff of dust kicking around us.

"I'm okay. Tired. Can you take this guy?" I nodded at the doctor, who had raised his head and was now eyeing Nate with trepidation.

"I've got him." Nate was dressed all in black, almost invisible against the inky blackness of the night. He grabbed the doctor by the scruff of the neck and hauled him to his feet.

"You have an SIA vehicle?" I coughed.

"Stole Carter's when I got your call."

"I called you?"

"Initially, I thought you were drunk, that you butt dialed me, didn't think much of it. Then, I heard on the news of your demise in a car explosion. And Carter had disappeared off the face of the earth at the same time. Didn't take a genius to figure the two of you had been taken. By Vince, I assumed."

"There's a cage in the back of the car. Put the doctor in it. I'll explain the rest after." I didn't want the doctor to be privy to our conversation. I released my hold on the doctor's ankle, grateful not to have to maintain the connection any longer. Nate hauled him to the car before returning to me seconds later.

"How did you know I was here?" I was dog-tired, my head was pounding, my knees were scraped from tumbling headfirst out of the window, and I'd never been happier to see anyone in my life.

"Let me see, one big ass explosion in an abandoned warehouse? Had your name all over it." He chuckled. "And I did not buy for one second that you'd been blown up in that car bomb. It stank like a cover-up engineered to stop anyone from looking for you. I've been systematically searching every abandoned warehouse on my list. I figured you were being held in one of them."

"Your list?"

"Carter had given a sample of the brick dust to Ethan. He came up with a list."

"I thought the SIA was working on that?"

"Carter said something about a backlog."

"More of Ridgeway's lies! She must have been trying to impede our investigation and slow us down by inventing a backlog in forensics. She's behind all of this." Struggling to my feet, I clenched his shirtfront in my fists to hold myself upright. I shivered in the cool night air, suddenly self-conscious in the thin cotton hospital gown I was wearing.

"Let's get you to the car." Scooping me up in his arms, ignoring my protest, Nate deposited me in the passenger seat of Carter's car within seconds before disappearing again.

"Are there any survivors?" Nate was back, carrying Carter, whom he laid on the back seat.

"I think we were the only ones inside when the blast went off, but I can't be sure. A group of guards had just arrived. They entered after the fire started. I'm not sure if they're still in there or if they got out."

He turned his gaze on me. "Have you seen Vince?"

"He was here earlier. He's the one who caught us. I think he was shot."

"Injured then. Probably hiding somewhere while he heals." Nate shot away, and I didn't protest at being left alone in the car with an unconscious Carter and the doctor under lock and key.

"Tell me what happened." Carter's groggy voice made me jump, and I swiveled in my seat to look at him.

"You're awake! Are you okay?"

"Now that I don't have them constantly pumping sedatives into my bloodstream." Grabbing my headrest, he pulled himself into a sitting position.

"More importantly, what about you?" He cupped

my cheek in his palm, his warmth soothing. "Vince beat you so badly. I thought he'd killed you."

"Nah." I tried to shrug it off, not wanting to relive the horror. "I'm okay. See?" I waved a hand at myself, indicating I was still in one piece. A little bruised and sore but not suffering any long-term ill effects.

"Raven, what did they do? How did they heal you? And don't lie to me, I know they did something because I heard your bones breaking each time Vince swung that fucking bat."

"They didn't do anything. I healed myself."

"What? How?" Carter was aware I had the healing capabilities of a human. Slow and limited.

"I'll explain it all later," I told him. "I heard a gunshot. Did she shoot him? I assume it was Ridgeway?"

"Yes, she shot him in the head. Pity it didn't kill him," Carter grumbled.

"What about you? What did they do to you?" I ran my hands over his face to assure myself he was in one piece.

"Shot me with another tranq dart when I went ballistic trying to get to you. I came to strapped on that bed. They were shoving the IV needle in. Fast-acting, whatever it was they used. I didn't wake up again until now."

"Specifically designed for wolves," the doctor said from his cage in the back. "You burn off tranquilizers so fast we had to develop a strong dose to bring you down initially, then keep it pumping into you intravenously to keep you down."

"Who's this guy?" Carter jerked his head to indicate the man in the back.

"He's the hired brains. He's been combining vampire venom and werewolf venom and injecting victims to try and make a superspecies."

"And they wanted you because?"

"They think because my species is undetermined that I'm the—I'm not sure, catalyst maybe? My DNA mixed with the vampires and the werewolves is the key."

"So they took more from you?"

I nodded. "Spinal fluid and blood. Which is why I'm a little shaky right now. They knew they could push me to the brink, and I'd survive. Heal."

"Shit." He cursed, "how did you get away?"

"I'll tell you later." I cocked my head to indicate the doctor, who was listening intently, although he was trying to look like he wasn't.

"I managed to get free, start a fire to destroy all of their samples and equipment, and I rescued him because he's my witness that Ridgeway is behind this."

I'd just finished telling my story when the driver's side door opened, and Nate slid in.

"No survivors. No, Vince. Let's go." Nate wiped the back of his hand across his mouth, cleaning away the drop of blood that clung to his lip. I suspected he'd drained the guards dry.

Nate started the SUV, and we headed out. I leaned my head back against the seat and closed my eyes, focusing on healing myself. I'd already learned that I couldn't heal as fast as a vampire or werewolf but faster than a human. In my mind's eye, I pictured the blood they'd drained from me, only this time, it was flowing back into my veins, the fluid they'd drained from my spine being replaced. I felt a sting in my back and winced, but then it settled, and I started to feel...better. The headache eased, my back stopped aching, and I no longer felt dizzy and weak.

"Why are we stopping here?" We'd been driving in silence, each of us lost in our thoughts, so when Nate suddenly pulled over and spoke, I jumped. We were almost at HQ.

"This is where I leave you."

"You should come in with us," I protested, swiveling to catch Nate's eyes. "We'll clear your name, I promise."

"Oh, my name will be cleared, don't worry." Nate's face was cold and expressionless, and I shivered. He was a man you did not want to make an enemy of. "I'm going to get Vince. He's pivotal in this whole thing. He's setting me up, and he can also dish the dirt on your director. This guy with the needles?" He jerked his head to indicate the scientist. "He can only give you so much. Enough to implicate Ridgeway, sure, but she's not behind the human auctions. She just bought produce from him. Bring Vince in, and you close two cases." Suddenly he smiled, a dimple flashing. "I see promotions in your futures." He chuckled, then let himself out of the car, the door closing almost silently.

"He's right." Carter climbed from the back of the car to the driver's seat. "It's not just Ridgeway we should be focusing on. Humans are still being taken, and the victims, were they part of an auction or specifically procured?"

"We need to order a team up to Wolf Hill. There may be a hunt in progress," I said. Carter was right. Suppose the victims were bought at auction, and Ridgeway had me under her control. In that case, she'd procure more humans, keen to accelerate her experiments.

A movement in the back of the vehicle caught my attention, and I looked at the doctor, who was looking out the window.

"What do you know?" I asked. His eyes darted to me, then away again. A shoulder hunched.

"Don't question him yet," Carter muttered.

"Why not?" I needed answers, and I needed them now. If there was another auction taking place, we needed to stop it. Or at least try to save the humans already sold.

"We need it on record." He kept his voice low. He was right. If we wanted any of this to stick, it had to be done through the appropriate channels; we had to record everything. I wondered if the director was at HQ and what would happen if we ran into her. Was she aware of the fire at the warehouse? Doubtful, unless one of the guards had alerted her before Nate took care of them.

At HQ, Carter took the doctor to an interview room while I retrieved a spare uniform from my locker and quickly showered. I stood for several seconds, staring at myself in the mirror. I looked the same. Nothing had changed, and yet, fundamentally, everything had. My thoughts touched briefly on the fire demon realm and if it were my heritage. I itched to find out, but it would have to wait.

***

THE DOCTOR'S name was Wesley Keller, and he was a biomedical engineer. He had nothing new to tell us, not that we didn't already know. But now we had it on record that Director Keri Ridgeway had hired him to engineer a new superspecies, and she had provided him with humans to experiment on. He also recounted how I'd built a firewall from nowhere, then an opening to pass through, then sent a fireball barreling through the warehouse, destroying everything.

"We need to delete the part about what I did. My new skills," I told Carter once we'd delivered Keller to the holding cells. "I don't need any more attention, from anyone, about what I can and can't do."

"Something else happened, didn't it?" Lacing his fingers with mine, he fell into step beside me.

"I think I know what I am. I'm a fire demon. Or at least part fire demon."

"You don't sound happy about it."

"I was abandoned as a baby, Carter. On purpose. Alone. Perhaps due to my fire demon status, or maybe because I'm part human; it doesn't matter. I was a baby!"

"Hey!" He stopped, cupping my face in his hands. "I appreciate you had a tough childhood, it wasn't easy for you, and you feel damaged because of it. But know this—you grew up into a beautiful, talented, strong woman."

"No thanks to my biological parents," I muttered, jerking my head out of his hands and continuing down the passageway.

"So...who are they? Do you know?"

I shook my head. "No. I need time to do more research. But I think maybe I'm related to the fire demon family in Maxxan. But can you keep that under your hat? I don't want anyone to know. I'm not ready for things to change just yet."

"You think they will? Once your species is known?" He sounded surprised, and I didn't blame him. I suspected nothing would change, but until the director was apprehended and anyone involved in her scheme dealt with, I couldn't trust word getting out. As it was, Keller hadn't been able to identify what I was.

"Until this case is closed and Ridgeway is apprehended, I say we keep it quiet."

"Fair enough."

We'd just reached the elevator when Carter's comms unit buzzed.

"Carter." He kept his eyes on me while he took the call. I took the opportunity to admire his handsome face, the stubble that was a little thicker than usual, the way his brows dipped down in a slight frown. Why was he frowning? I dragged my attention back to his call.

"Put Wilder in one interview room, Santiago in another. We'll be right there."

"Nate found him." I couldn't suppress the smile spreading across my face.

"We've got a problem." Carter's somber words wiped the smile right off.

"What's that?"

"The director. We're closing in on her. We can't have her finding out we have her doctor or Santiago in custody. We also don't know if anyone here is working for her. It's risky."

"Do you think she'd send someone to silence them? Before they could talk? But we've already got everything we need from Keller. She's well and truly implicated."

"Yes, but if she's got someone on the inside, witnesses can be silenced and evidence destroyed. We need to move fast on this. She's in a position of power, and that could work against us. Word will spread quickly now that we've got Vince Santiago in custody."

Carter was right. Ridgeway had a lot of power in the SIA, and she used it to her advantage.

"You question Vince," I said. "Do you have your phone on you?" He nodded, pulling it out of his pocket. "Good. Call me. Keep the connection open. We need a backup in case Ridgeway does destroy any audio and video. Get Vince talking about her. Get as much as you can out of him."

I went to pull out my phone only to realize I didn't have it. It had been smashed on a footpath out in front of my apartment and then planted in my bombed car. Shit! Then an idea hit me. Stepping into the elevator with Carter, I laid out my plan. I'd borrow Nate's phone, keep him isolated with instructions not to talk to anyone, to appear uncooperative. Carter would contact fellow enforcers McConnell, Richards, Augustine, and Darabi and tell them we'd apprehended Nate Wilder. One of them, if not all, would pass the word around, and hopefully, the fuss over having Nate in custody would hide the fact that we also had Vince.

"What will you be doing?" Carter asked when we arrived at our destination. He stepped out of the lift while I remained inside, holding the doors open.

"Besides recording everything Vince says, I'm going to the Council. Ridgeway could swoop in here and cut Vince loose, destroy evidence, do whatever she wants. We need a higher power to issue an arrest warrant for her, to revoke all access. We don't have time to file reports and put in written requests."

"You think the Council will see you?"

"I have an in. George Kane has spoken with me before. I'm sure he will again. And he already knows that Ridgeway illegally ordered tests on me."

"Yeah, but he did nothing about that."

"That we know of. Things could have been happening behind the scenes." I wanted to give George the benefit of the doubt. He'd seemed surprised and concerned when I'd told him what had been happening. He'd said he'd investigate the incident, and I assumed he would keep true to his word.

"Wait for my call," I said. "I'm getting Nate's

phone out of evidence. It'll take me a couple of minutes."

"I'll visit him first, let him in on our plan. And don't worry"—he held up his hand to silence me when I opened my mouth to interrupt—"I'll be discreet. The camera won't pick it up." Stepping up to me, he wrapped a hand around my nape and tugged me toward him, his lips landing on mine.

And just like every other time he kissed me, all thoughts left my head. That we were on a time crunch, most likely in danger, none of it mattered. All that mattered at this moment was his mouth on mine, the taste of him on my tongue. I growled, and he chuckled, slowly backing away. Reluctantly I let him go. Dropping my hand from the elevator door, I kept my gaze locked on his until the door slid closed between us.

TWENTY-ONE

awn was streaking the sky with pink and lavender when I left the SIA. Standing in front of my apartment, I stifled a yawn. The last twenty-four hours had been surreal. Drugged and kidnapped by Vince, who was working for the director, discovering I was a fire demon, watching in awe as the Council took control of the SIA, issuing an arrest warrant for the director, clearing Nate of all charges, and making the human hunts our priority. The Council operated like a well-oiled machine, and I had to give them credit for it. I'd always considered the council as figureheads, pencil pushers who didn't bring much value to the paranormal community beyond being simple puppets for their respective species. How wrong was I?

There were layers to the Council no one was aware of. They had their own secret service, soldiers trained in war. I couldn't believe the SIA hadn't known about them, but I guess that was the point. In situations like ours, where someone in a position of power becomes corrupt.

Carter, looking like he'd been through a war zone, wrapped an arm around me as the sun's fingers banished the dark. "Pretty, isn't it?" he murmured, watching the sunrise with a weariness that mirrored my own.

"I've seen worse," I quipped, leaning into his side. Our shared exhaustion was a blanket, heavy and warm, but our world wouldn't allow the luxury of rest. Not yet.

"I'm beat," he admitted, and I chuckled. "Me too."

There was so much more to talk about, so much more to sort out, but exhaustion tugged at us. We'll talk later.

Later came sooner than anticipated. I'd been asleep for what felt like minutes when there was a banging at my front door. Shuffling downstairs in a tank and sweats, I brushed away tangles of hair and flung open the door with a scowl. Nate, fist poised to hammer again, shouldered past me with a grin that didn't reach his eyes. "Morning, sunshine. Eggs?"

"What do you want?" Closing the front door, I followed. "And did you bring breakfast?"

"I didn't, but I'll make you something." He grinned, opening my fridge door and peering inside. "How do you like your eggs?"

"Prepared by someone else," I grumbled, climbing onto a barstool and watching as he placed the eggs on the counter and fixed coffee. "What do you want?" I asked again.

"I have a feeling what I'm about to say is going to piss you off." He stopped what he was doing and faced me, arms crossed over his chest. *Great. Now what?*

"Just spit it out. I'm tired. I've had what? Three hours of sleep? I'm not in the mood for word games or dancing around the topic."

"So I'm the temporary Director of the SIA," he said, watching me closely. Okay. Not what I was expecting, but I shrugged; so what? Someone had to be. May as well be him.

"You have no SIA experience," I pointed out.

"They wanted someone clean. New. With my

special ops background and the resources I have at my disposal…"

"Yeah, fine, whatever." I cut him off. I really didn't care. Unless he was about to fire me. "Wait! You're not firing me, are you?"

Laughing, he shook his head. "No, I'm not firing you. Or Carter," he added before I could ask. Right on cue, Carter appeared at the top of the stairs.

"What do you want?" He sounded as grumpy as me. I smiled, leaning in for a kiss when he slid onto the stool beside me.

Nate continued making the coffee, sliding two steaming mugs across the counter to us.

"He's here to tell me something that's going to piss me off." I updated Carter, taking a sip of my coffee.

"Oh?" Carter cradled his mug and watched Nate with narrowed eyes.

"How about the good news first?" Nate looked at a spot just beyond my shoulder. He was nervous. Which made me nervous. What did he have to say that was so terrible?

"Spit it out." Carter missed the undercurrents, eyes on his coffee instead.

"The night you two were taken. There was no human auction. So we don't have any more missing humans. And with Vince on lockdown, the ring has been disbanded."

"That's good." I nodded, still on edge. "What else?"

"By combining resources, we made significant headway in determining Ridgeway's plans."

"We know her plans. To make a *super* supernatural."

"I meant why she chose those particular humans. They were specifically chosen. Vince told us she gave him the names. They weren't random. And they were kidnapped off the streets, not as part of an auction sweep which consisted of snatching the homeless."

"I'll bite. Why those particular humans? And where are my eggs?"

Rummaging around in my cupboards, Nate retrieved a bowl and began breaking eggs into it. "Because all of the victims have the Cennit6 gene. It's rare. Very rare."

"Okay. That's not news. Our lab confirmed something about a rare gene." I shrugged.

"From Keller's notes, we can see that he believes that gene is the key to a successful mutation, but they needed—a bridge, so to speak, to successfully marry that gene to the paranormal DNA."

"Okay." I nodded. I didn't know much about genes, DNA, and science, but what he said sounded feasible.

"You're the bridge."

"Okay," I said again. I already figured they thought my DNA was the key.

"Buried deep in your DNA, you have what they call building blocks. Well, they don't really call them that. They have a long scientific name I can't pronounce, but the gist of it is, they are building blocks."

"And what does that mean? Precisely?"

"It means you can mix any other DNA with yours and create a hybrid species. You know how vampires can't be born; they're created? By one vampire turning another? And werewolves and shifters are born, not created through a bite or a scratch? Your DNA turns all that on its head. You can give birth to a vampire baby. You can give birth to a werewolf or shifter baby."

Riiiiiight. A thought drifted across my mind about the first time I'd had sex with Carter and how pissed I'd been that we hadn't used protection. Seems my sixth sense was bang on.

I squared my shoulders, eyes locked on Nate's,

searching for the flicker of truth. "So Keller was right then. I am the key. But why would that piss me off?"

Nate's gaze didn't waver. "We know what you are, Raven. The Council knows."

The words slammed into me. "What?!" How could they know when I wasn't a hundred percent sure myself?

"You're a fire demon," Nate said, voice steady, watching the shock ripple across my face.

The room spun. Carter spilled his coffee, cursing under his breath. "How did they find out?"

I could barely think, barely breathe. "How?" I echoed, voice barely above a whisper.

Nate leaned in, his voice carrying the weight of secrets and the fire that burned within me. "They've always known, Raven. Since the day you were born."

The revelation slung through the air like a stray bullet, finding its home in the pit of my stomach. I was predestined for this mess, a marked woman from my first cry. It wasn't just the SIA or the Council. It was me, the epicenter of an inevitable cataclysm, labeled and filed away as a 'just in case' by powers that watched from the shadows.

Carter's hand found mine, his grip firm, grounding. "So, we're what? Supernatural royalty now?" He tried for a joke, but his voice was strained, the humor falling flat in the tense kitchen.

"More like supernatural guinea pigs," I corrected, the bitterness in my tone surprising even me. I squeezed his hand back, a silent promise—I wouldn't let this newfound title dictate our lives.

Nate cleared his throat, shifting uneasily. "The Council asked me to give you this." Nate handed over an official document, complete with a red seal. Tearing it open, I read it, then looked at him in disbelief.

"What does it say?" Carter leaned over, trying to read the paper in my hands.

"They want me on the Council. To represent the fire demons. My species." It was ridiculous, of course. I wasn't even a full-fire demon. I was part human; therefore, I didn't qualify to serve on the Council.

"No thanks." I tossed the paper back at Nate.

"Would she have to leave the SIA?" Carter asked at the same time. Nate turned his attention to Carter and nodded. "Yes. But I have a sweetener."

"Oh?"

"Positions for both of you on the SS. Secret Supernaturals."

"No," I responded immediately. I liked my job at

the SIA. I liked my colleagues. I liked my life. This was all too much.

Carter grabbed my wrist to hold me in place when I went to slide off my barstool. "Think about it for a second, Raven. You—we—could do a lot of good, especially if you're on the Council."

"It's ridiculous they'd offer me a position on the Council," I scoffed. "I'm human. It's a waste of everyone's time."

Nate's eyes held mine, a silent promise that the truth would reshape everything I knew. "You're not human, Raven. Not in the way anyone would expect."

I frowned, confusion and frustration swirling. "But every test, every scan shows I'm human. One hundred percent."

"That's the thing," Nate leaned in, his voice dropping to a near-whisper, "your DNA—it's a masterpiece of disguise. It's fire demon through and through, but it's cloaked, hidden beneath a human veil. That's part of your ability, your unique heritage."

I shook my head, trying to comprehend. "But how? If I'm a full-blood fire demon, how am I not... on fire or something?"

Nate chuckled softly, the sound strangely

comforting. "Fire demons aren't just about literal fire, Raven. It's about an inner strength, a power more than flame. It's about survival, resilience. Your parents were both full-blooded fire demons. And they were part of a lineage that believed in coexistence with humans, which is why they chose to blend in, to live and love as humans do."

"The Sheltons in Maxxan," I whispered, the puzzle pieces clicking into place. "They're…"

"Distant relatives," Nate confirmed. "Your family's history is complicated, tangled with human and demon worlds. Your parents were visionaries. They wanted a future where their kind could live openly, without fear."

"And they died for it," I murmured, the weight of centuries of hiding and fear pressing down on me. "Didn't they?"

Nate reached out, his hand enveloping mine. "They died protecting you, Raven. You were their hope, a bridge between two worlds. Your existence challenges the very nature of our reality—what it means to be a demon, a human, a creature of the night. And that's why you were hidden away, why your DNA was designed to deceive any who looked too closely."

I sat back, the enormity of Nate's words

wrapping around me like a cloak. I was a full-blood fire demon with the power to upend the natural order, to create life in ways that defied explanation. The key to a future where lines didn't divide species but united them.

"Oh my God." I dropped my head into my hands. Even though the parchment in front of me was an invitation, I knew it was a thinly veiled order. Refusal was not an option.

"There's another positive," Carter whispered, his breath hot against my ear.

I looked at him out of the corner of my eye. "Do tell," I muttered, not at all enthused at this turn of events.

"It could get the pack off our backs. If my mate was not only on the Council but also able to birth wolves?" His words hung heavy in the silence. It was true. I was sure the pack would welcome me with open arms if my status changed from that of an ordinary SIA agent to a member of the Council. As for the other? "They'd be hybrid babies," I pointed out.

"But with all of the traits of both species. Am I right, Nate? If we had a baby, it would have all my wolf abilities?"

"Correct. And Raven's abilities."

"Powerful," Carter breathed.

"Yeah, don't get too excited," I shot him down. "We're not creating a mini-army. We're talking about having babies. Can you see me with a baby? I'm not exactly maternal." How had we gotten on this topic? Panic washed through me, knowing Carter's pack, heck, any wolf pack, was all about reproduction. That was why I wasn't suitable in their eyes. Would they welcome hybrid offspring into their pack? I couldn't bear to bring a child into the world that was shunned as I was.

"They would love, cherish, and protect any child we produced." Carter swiveled me to face him, hands on my shoulders. "If we had a child, they would welcome it. They're just overprotective of me, but if we had a kid? It would be loved."

"I'm not getting out of this, am I?" I turned my attention back to Nate.

"The Council needs you, and your people need you. And as the acting Director of SIA, it would help me to have a friendly ear on Council." He winked, and I couldn't hold back the snort of laughter. Of course, there was something in it for him.

"I guess I'm joining the Council. Now, about those eggs?"

TWENTY-TWO

Standing in front of the full-length mirror in my rooms at the Council, I smoothed my palms over the flowing navy fabric draped around my shoulders. The cloak with its golden trim was the official ceremonial robe of the Council. Tonight was my swearing-in ceremony. I'd agreed to their proposal on the proviso I had a six-month probationary period. After six months, if I didn't like it, I could leave with no repercussions, and likewise, if they felt I wasn't the right fit, they could remove me from the Council.

Neither of those things happened. We'd had plenty of volatile moments, and I'd walked out of more than one meeting due to members bickering over inconsequential matters. In the past, it was customary for them to waste inordinate amounts of time on trivial topics. I didn't have time for that. I now had more than one hundred fire demons transitioning into life on Earth. Decisions needed to be made quickly.

Apparently, the Council liked my fiery brand of diplomacy and my no-holds-barred way of telling them what they didn't want to hear. I shook things up and challenged the status quo, something no one had dared do in the past. I was a hit.

My hands settled on the swell of my stomach, and I smiled at the irony. Not only was I serving on the Council and loving it, but I was also knocked up. Two things I had never, in my wildest dreams, imagined happening.

The door behind me opened, and Carter stepped inside, his footsteps silent on the plush carpeting. Each Council member had a suite of rooms beneath the council chambers, containing a bedroom, bathroom, sitting room, and a small kitchenette. I'd taken to hanging out here whenever Carter worked late with the SS. He, too, had taken to his new role like a duck to water. He loved the undercover assignments he got sent on, and liaising with Nate at the SIA had helped relations between the two departments now that the SS wasn't so secret.

"You look amazing," he said, his voice a soft echo in the chambers of my anxious heart.

I feigned exasperation, "I look ridiculous in navy, and this thing weighs a ton." But my reflection betrayed me, lips quivering on the brink of a smile.

"It's only for a while, love," he chuckled, and then, with the tender reverence of a man who held his world in his arms, he closed the space between us. His arms encircled me, a gentle fortress, his hands resting with a whisper's touch upon the life we'd created.

In the mirror, I watched as the man who'd become my unexpected everything, the secret keeper of my heart, smoothed a strand of hair back with a touch that spoke of shared secrets and nights entwined in whispers.

This embrace wasn't just an embrace—it was a vow, a silent promise that echoed the depth of our shared solitude, our united front against the world's chaos. It was Carter saying, without words, that we were in this—this life, this moment, this surreal and beautiful mess—together.

And in the reflection, I saw not just a woman donned in the heavy trappings of her new role but a heart, fiercely guarded and fiercely loving, standing ready to face whatever came next.

"I admit, I feel a little nervous." My eyes caught his in the mirror.

"Of the ceremony?" he asked in surprise. I shook my head. No. The ceremony was just a formality, and on some things, I had to bend and do what the rest of the Council wanted. A ball was being held in my honor, officially welcoming me into the Council. That part I was okay with. It was after.

"I don't think they're going to take it well," I said, twisting my engagement ring around and around on my finger. Carter had proposed to me a week after we'd blown Director Ridgeway's diabolical plan out of the water. Unfortunately, she'd fled town, and we'd yet to locate her. Distracted with the hunt for Ridgeway, I'd turned him down. Undeterred, he continued to propose every week until I caved and said yes. And then I discovered I was pregnant. His pack had thawed toward me when they learned how compatible my species was. They'd softened a little more when Carter had told them we were engaged. They were positively welcoming when we announced my pregnancy. They'd been madly planning our wedding ever since.

"They're going to be hurt," I fretted. The last thing I wanted was to hurt his pack.

"They'll get over it. And why are you hiding this away?" Tugging on the gold chain around my neck, he pulled it from beneath my dress, revealing the simple golden band threaded through the chain. "This should be on your finger. You are, after all, my wife."

"I know. And I couldn't be happier. I swear." He removed the ring from the chain and slid it on my finger, where it nestled perfectly against the diamond engagement ring.

"You've gotten soft, Black," he said, caressing my chin with his knuckles. It was true. I had. Carter and I had married in secret last night. The whole wedding planning chaos had been creating too much stress, and since neither of us cared about a big wedding, we'd eloped. Only the Council knew. And tonight, we'd announce it to everyone.

A knock at the door distracted me from my worries over the pack. It was time. Opening the door, I was taken aback to see Nate standing there, resplendent in a black tux, a brown paper bag held up in one hand.

"What?" I laughed at the goofy expression on his face.

"Usually, you open the door demanding to know what I've brought for breakfast. I didn't want to disappoint." Handing me the bag, he stepped over the threshold.

"It's not breakfast time, Nate," I chided, opening the bag and peeking inside. A bacon and egg burger greeted me. Unwrapping the burger, I took a bite.

"Pregnancy hasn't changed your appetite, I see." Nate grinned, walking past to slap Carter on the shoulder in greeting.

"If anything, it's doubled it," Carter said. It was true. I was constantly hungry.

"What are you doing here, Nate?" I asked around a mouthful of burger.

"Came to escort you upstairs for the ceremony. You know you get a crown and this motherfucking medallion that's enormous. I mean, it's almost the size of my head."

"What?" I coughed, choking. Carter slapped me on the back and punched Nate in the shoulder. "He's winding you up, babe."

"Asshole," I muttered, finishing the burger and wiping my mouth on the napkin at the bottom of the bag.

"No, but seriously." Nate stepped up to me and rubbed my cheek with his thumb. I assumed I had food stuck to my face. "I wanted to thank you for everything. Right from the start, you believed in me.

You could have arrested me multiple times, but you didn't, and having you on my side...well...it means a lot."

"Are you getting mushy on me, Wilder?" I cocked my head, not sure if he was serious.

"I think I might be," he admitted, hanging his head.

"Come here, you big lug." I pulled him into a hug. He'd become a friend to Carter and me, and he was doing good things at the SIA. "You're a dear friend, and I do my best not to arrest my friends. No matter how much of a pain in the ass they are."

"I can't believe you're allowed on the Council with that potty mouth." Nate laughed.

"They love it. I think. Anyway, which one of you is escorting me? May as well go and make this official!" I stood, twisting my hands in the fabric of my cloak, my heart rate skyrocketing at what was about to unfold.

Carter's hands found my shoulders, a gentle pressure that settled the frantic beating of my heart. His arms wrapped around me, a shield against the weight of what was to come. I lingered a moment, a rare stillness in our world of constant motion. The importance of the cloak felt like history settling on my shoulders, a tangible reminder of the duty I'd shouldered — not just for the fire demons, but for the life growing inside me, Carter, and the pack waiting for our news.

I remembered the escape clause, that little backdoor I'd demanded, a reminder of who I'd been six months ago: someone always ready to run. Now, it seemed frivolous. I wasn't the same person who needed a way out. I'd become someone who planted her feet firmly and faced whatever came. This ceremony wasn't just an induction; it was a celebration of permanence, of roots finally taking hold in soil I never thought I'd call home.

Nate's joke about the crown and medallion, a tease or not, reminded me that even the heaviest regalia didn't compare to the weight of responsibility I'd willingly taken on. And I was ready to bear it — with a partner who knew me, a friend who respected me, and a pack that was learning to accept me.

So when Nate and Carter took their places at my sides, it wasn't just an escort to a ceremony; it was a march towards a future I was ready to embrace, no escape clause needed. Because for the first time, I didn't want one.

Ready for more? Join Rae and Jordan in **Stalk the Night**, where the pulse of the paranormal beats even stronger, and every decision could alter the fabric of their world.
Grab your copy of Stalk the Night here:
www.JaneHinchey.com/Enforcers

Thank you for reading! If you enjoyed this book, I'd greatly appreciate your review.

You can find a complete list of my books, including series and reading order on my website at:

www.JaneHinchey.com

Join my newsletter here:

www.JaneHinchey.com/subscribe

And finally, join my readers group on Facebook here:

www.JaneHinchey.com/LittleDevils

Thank you so much for taking a chance and reading my book . It's readers like you who make this journey worthwhile and fuel my passion for storytelling. Your support means the world to me, and I can't wait to share more exciting stories with you in the future.

xoxo

Jane

FREE BOOK OFFER

Want to get an email alert when a new book is released?

Sign up for my newsletter today,

https://janehinchey.com/subscribe

and as a bonus, receive a FREE e-book of

Cupcakes & Curses!

READ MORE BY JANE

Find them all at www.JaneHinchey.com/books

The Ghost Detective Mysteries

#1 Ghost Mortem

#2 Give up the Ghost

#3 The Ghost is Clear

#4 A Ghost of a Chance

#5 Here Ghost Nothing

#6 Who Ghost There?

#7 Wild Ghost Chase

#8 Easy Come, Easy Ghost

#9 Life Ghost On

Witch Way Paranormal Cozy Mystery Series

#1 Witch Way to Magic & Mayhem

#2 Witch Way to Romance & Ruin

#3 Witch Way Down Under

#4 Witch Way to Beauty & the Beach

#5 Witch Way to Death & Destruction

#6 Witch Way to Secrets & Sorcery

<u>The Gravestone Mysteries</u>

#1 Fur the Hex of it

#2 Battle of the Hexes

#3 What the Hex

<u>The Midnight Chronicles</u>

#1 One Minute to Midnight

#2 Two Minutes Past Midnight

#3 Third Strike of Midnight

<u>Clean Scene Inc.</u>

#1 All in Vein

PARANORMAL ROMANCE/URBAN FANTASY

The Awakening Trilogy

Hell's Angel Trilogy

The Enforcer Series (4 books)

Standalones

Returned

Secret Fates

Destiny's Touch

Blood Cursed

Heart of Darkness

ABOUT JANE

Hi there! I'm Jane, crafting tales of paranormal cozy mysteries sprinkled with urban fantasy romance. Between sips of coffee and dodging my mischievous cats, I immerse myself in stories where magic meets everyday life.

Once known as Zahra Stone in the world of steamy urban fantasy, I've now merged those fiery tales under the Jane Hinchey banner. Off the page you'll find me binging on true crime documentaries or sneaking in a power nap. Dive into my stories and join me on an enchanting journey!

Find me here: www.janehinchey.com

facebook.com/janehincheyauthor

instagram.com/janehincheyauthor

amazon.com/Jane-Hinchey/e/B0193449MI

bookbub.com/authors/jane-hinchey

goodreads.com/jane_hinchey

www.ingramcontent.com/pod-product-compliance
Lightning Source LLC
Chambersburg PA
CBHW051251210726

48287CB00002B/452